EMAIL FROM THE FUTURE

Notes from 2084

ALSO BY MICHAEL ROGERS

Mindfogger
Do Not Worry About the Bear
Biohazard
Silicon Valley
Forbidden Sequence

For Donna Rini

A map of the world that does not include Utopia is not worth glancing at.
—OSCAR WILDE

It is certainly the fate of all Utopias to be more or less misread.
—H.G. WELLS

PRACTICAL
FUTURIST®

This book is a work of fiction. Any references to historical events, real people or real places are used fictitiously. Other names, characters, places, and events are products of the author's imagination, and any resemblance to actual events or places or persons, living or dead, is entirely coincidental.

Interior design by Ray Shappell

ISBN 978-0-578-35537-5

EMAIL FROM THE FUTURE

Posted October 14, 2020

Email from the Future?

As regular readers of this blog have heard before, when you're a futurist, you receive strange email.

Perhaps that's because we futurists are the last generalists. We tend to know a little about a lot of stuff, and we try to piece it together. So if you're a disgruntled citizen who wants to rant about kids these days, or Apple software updates, or the state of healthcare…well, the people who could do something about your problem probably just ignore you.

But then you find a blogger or a YouTuber who actually talks about how these things might change, and you think: maybe they'll listen. Worth a try!

So, I get a lot of strange, but occasionally interesting, email. Last week a particularly large message appeared in my inbox.

The subject line on the email was simply "TXT." And that was accurate: It was a very long document in plain text, one giant run-on page, no paragraph breaks, only occasionally punctuated, words sometimes run together, a bizarre unbroken digital rant. A real pain to reformat into readable prose.

I was about to delete, but for some reason I stopped, and began to repair the first page or two. Why? Idle curiosity.

Plus, we're in the middle of the COVID lockdown and I have plenty of time on my hands.

After I read a bit, I realized that this was an unusual piece of writing. I finished reformatting and then did some digital forensics on the original email.

The sender address is null@null.com which is, of course, a meaningless spoof. There's also almost no other origin information attached to the email: no message id, no mime version, none of the standard digital identifiers that even the most clumsily-faked email would normally carry.

I know what the security-minded among you are thinking: it wasn't an email, it was inserted via some strange new hack. By now I've run three different malware detectors on my computer. No virus, no backdoors, nothing out of the ordinary.

In short, I'm not certain how this found its way onto my desktop.

However, I've now read the whole document. Someone went to quite a bit of work for no clear reward.

Someone apparently named Aldus, who claims he is living in Brooklyn right now. (The only Aldus I can locate in New York City is a street in the Bronx.)

I'll post the entire piece below. Readers can make of it what they will.

And Aldus, if you happen to see this, please do send me another email. But this time, try to use some punctuation.

Click here to download "TXT" (540 KB)

JUNE 2084

Thursday, June 2

The idea to write these essays came to me two weeks ago, as I stood beside your mother, late on a crisp Ohio afternoon in the spring of 2084. I was watching you, my only grandchild, toss the ashes of your dream list into the cold, clear waters of the Scioto River, at the edge of New Williamsburg.

You are about to turn five, and it was a day of firsts for you. It was your first 350 Day celebration, the first time you'd been allowed to burn your wishes yourself. You even wrote—well, scribbled—them with your own hands, your first experience with graphite and natural paper.

Dozens of other families surrounded us on the newly green riverbank for the Wishes Toss. There was music and food and a big black metal pan—the "wishes foundry"—where all the children's folded pages were burned.

The excitement of the day had you flushed and giggling. They say you resemble me, but I am 70 years older than you, and to my eye I resemble no one except, perhaps, Father Time.

You craned your neck as we watched the ashes disappear downstream; you wanted to keep them in view just as long as possible, although they were already invisible. But I could imagine the ashes traveling down the Scioto, out into the Ohio River, then merging into the Mississippi, through the new National Park, and finally, seventy kilometers west of New Orleans, coursing into the 2032 Atchafalaya Flood channel and out to the Gulf of Mexico. The carbonized fragments of your wishes will pass through more than a thousand kilometers of healthy land once tormented by floods, chemicals, droughts, toxic algae.

Your mother Sofia asked softly: "Luca, what does 350 Day mean?"

You replied quickly: "Wishes come true!"

"But why today?"

You returned to earth for a moment. "Uh...it means we fixed the air!"

"And much more," Sofia said. "It means anything is possible. Ask your grandfather. Nonno was there."

Well. Of course you didn't ask me at the time—what five-year-old celebrating his first 350 Day would, when the food is being put out and the lasers about to paint the dusk?

In a few years, the day may come when you do ask, perhaps urged by Tutor: "This weekend, ask an elder what the War was like, and we will talk about it on Monday."

But I might no longer be there to answer. Ironic, considering that my generation will be the first regularly to live beyond 100. Media tell us that one's seventies are now middle age and we have decades of active life ahead.

It may be so. But even with the formidable medical tools of today, all the genomic interventions and neural implants and replica organs, there are still disorders we cannot heal. And I may be one of the unlucky ones, carrying a nasty bit of our unhappy early century that still lingers in a few unfortunates of my generation.

I still clearly remember the joy of the first 350 Day, May 15, 2049, when the planet's carbon level had averaged three hundred fifty parts per million for a full year. Certainly, three hundred fifty was still too high and most of the Warming's impacts remained, but there was a collective burst of confidence. The goal was three hundred, which had been the global average in 1900. In the decades since the first 350 Day, the capture factories and global regreening continued the drawdown so dependably that when we reached three hundred a decade ago, little fuss was made.

During the 2020s and 2030s, at the height of the Warming, the global birthrate had dropped precipitously—floods, famines, fires, droughts, mass migration. Even in the wealthy countries, where suffering was less, there was a contagious climate angst among the young.

Why launch children into a future that appeared so tentative and perilous? Most people we knew chose to freeze. And it was not just a lack of desire to bear children—the fertility rate declined significantly, for reasons not fully understood, most probably stress-related. Nature itself didn't want more babies.

But in 2049 we knew that we were going to win the War. And the result was, as one humorist put it, a run on the egg banks.

I was thirty-nine, your grandmother Marianna was thirty-seven, and we were living in a townhouse in New Williamsburg. Your father was born almost exactly nine months after that first 350 Day, an early arrival in the largest generation since those misunderstood Millennials.

Everyone, of course, was choosing optimistic baby names. And so that's why your father is named Dylan, after a Nobel Prize-winning songwriter from the famously optimistic 1960s. (Maybe archaic names are a family trait; my name, Aldus, comes from the 15th century printer who created the form of the modern book.)

In a few years you'll learn all our century's history from Tutor. So why do I feel the need to repeat it?

You will turn twenty-one in the first year of the 22nd century. A fresh page to inscribe. You and your generation have known no society other than this one, which we now find mostly pleasing and just. Problems remain, of course, and much work is yet to be done, but it feels as if our species has arrived at some benign plateau.

For now. Time is never kind to contentment, and we don't know what lies ahead.

But this is about what has already gone right: the transformation of our species and the planet in the 21st century, starting when the outlook was dire, and what it was like to be there.

In the early century, when I was your age, we had the technologies, the social models, the economic understandings...all the tools we needed to make the planet a healthy and just place to live.

As a species, we simply needed to do everything right for fifty years or so.

Did we do everything right? Of course not.

But we were close enough.

What I write won't be instructional; you'll learn enough

facts from Tutor. Neither is this a memoir; that would be pompous and unwarranted. You'll see many biographies of my generation's greats, and I was, at best, a foot soldier. But there is also value in the soldier's perspective.

And of course my media is tagged for Lifepath, so you'll have that also.

I refuse to sit for a Simula, although I know it's all the rage among people my age. I can't bear the thought of an AI avatar of myself, some digital doppelgänger prattling on, a decade after my passing. It would be a cheap and tawdry souvenir, telling you little of my essence. Your parents agree with me on this but if, a decade hence, all your friends have Simulacrum grandparents and you have none, just tell them your Nonno was irredeemably old-fashioned. And then count yourself lucky that you have these words from me rather than a glowing shapeshifting blob of bloviating AI.

Writing is a skill I achieved late in life, and this how I want to leave my words, even if it's the static language you'll call a fossil document. Fossils have taught our species a great deal. And for me, writing is still a unique medium: the thought travels straight to word, and then the word returns directly to thought. Even today, no neural link is as precise as the well-chosen word.

The essay is a literary form best suited to freehand writing, so I will take that as my challenge. And there will be family history, when I can't resist.

Please bear with me as I choose my words. I might ramble a bit in the telling, but we are certain to arrive at an end.

And may you read this in an even better world than we have today.

MY GENERATION

By the time I was ten years old, in 2020, Generation Z already had an unfortunate reputation. Most adults expected us Zoomers to grow up to be idiots, addicted to the virtual world, consuming meaningless content day and night.

Now your generation hears instead all sorts of heroic bravado about our role in the War on the Warming; the War has inspired contemporary storytellers in the same way that World War II did 20th century writers and filmmakers. And in the retellings, the War has become an idealized, swash-buckling romantic era, and Gen Z is called the "Boldest Generation." Actually, I think we should be called the Resilient Generation—that's the quality that describes us best.

But heroes make better stories than survivors. When your father was ten or eleven, for example, he loved a VR adventure game called *Flood Team 2035,* about a team of flood recovery specialists, UniServ recruits from around the world. It followed seven characters in their late teens and 20s through the great floods of the 2030s—New Jersey, upper Bangladesh, the Mississippi basin, central California, northern India, and all the others. (No one I knew actually saw that much frontline service during the War. Actual rescue was done mostly by military units, supported by UniServ. Most UniServ recruits would be rotated out after even one major flood mission.)

The characters in *FT35* ranged from Kevin, an eighteen-year-old recruit fresh out of Montana to Kia, a tough Filipina engineer in her late twenties, on her third service rotation. The variety of backgrounds was accurate; disaster recovery teams were always a mix of nationalities.

FT35 had a famous romance, between Kia and Jiao, a young woman volunteer from China whom everyone called "Princess." She was a slightly unlikely character, Chinese ultrarich; until the Soft Revolution in the 2050s, China maintained a harsh and highly stratified class system. (Some of the more idealistic Chinese ultrarich did volunteer for Uniserv, which is credited by historians for planting the seeds of the Soft Revolution.)

People somehow can't forget that romance, played out against the chaotic and dangerous flood work. You might even hear "Kia and Jiao" the way that people my age heard "Romeo and Juliet."

In the final scene, Kia and Jiao are in Uttar Pradesh airlifting German carbon fiber levees into place, and Kia is bitten by a bamboo pit viper. She refuses evacuation, choosing instead to lock the last few meters of levee into their moorings just as the next rain bomb hits—and then she succumbs to the venom moments before assistance arrives.

Sentimental melodrama, I know, but it's the Gen-Z hagiography your father's generation grew up with. The FT35 gameplay is ancient now, but I wouldn't be surprised if you watch the narrative when you're a bit older. While your generation still has challenges ahead—rewilding, reef restoration, national boundaries, global Living Income—they are not the against-all-odds physical adventure of the early War on the Warming.

We Zs are remembered collectively as bold heroes. But what choice did we have? We grew up into a collapsing planet, vast international income inequality, systemic racism, few real employment opportunities, and in the US, costly educations and a capricious and mercenary healthcare system. We were the precariat generation, often at best destined for corporate "gig work." And even that would soon be eaten away by automation.

Those were depressing times; by the mid-2020s Gen Z had the highest suicide rate of any young generation. Adults blamed it on the internet. We should have said: How about blaming it on the world you're leaving us?

And the Millennials—who were supposed to be the great hope for the new century—had gotten *old.* At least they looked awfully old to Zoomers. Many Millennials had finally managed to start careers and families, bought little starter homes, cobbling together four different jobs to pay the mortgage. Some even started using Facebook! (Early century joke…you will study the Facebook era with Tutor.) While the Millennials still faced difficult futures, the corporate powers had tossed them enough crumbs to feed the delusion that the system might still work.

So it was up to my generation to act. We were, after all, the first generation that practiced political demonstrations in grade school. We were excused from class for climate rallies. Our parents had taken us to the early century racial equity protests.

Historians now compare our rising anger and strength in the 2020s to the energy of the 1960s: an old order breaking apart, a new vision emerging. Of course, in the 1960s that energy was quickly coopted by the corporate powers, and for most, the economics of life actually became worse.

* * *

Even with the energy of my generation, it was years before the War on Warming truly began.

The 2020s started as another decade of climate change meetings and conferences. There was fresh optimism following a change in leadership in the United States, so the governments and corporate powers churned out even more promises and pledges. Pledges sometimes met, sometimes not, but never enough to truly reverse the rise of carbon in our atmosphere.

The truth was that the governments of the world had lost control; they could legislate and regulate all they wanted, but the corporate powers and the ultrarich, from New York and Beijing to Moscow and Jeddah, made the decisions. The level of carbon dioxide in the atmosphere continued to rise, even as new decarbonization technology emerged, and the cost of renewable energy dropped.

Students today ask: Why didn't the people demand action?

It's important to remember that in the early 2020s, the majority of humans were still born closer to 1960 than 2000. The worst consequences of the Warming were in a future they likely wouldn't experience. Many were in denial, unable to accept the fact that they were leaving their grandchildren a sickly, dying, plundered planet, far diminished from the Earth they had inherited. Others believed in climate change but had been persuaded there was time for gradual solutions. And the corporate powers happily sustained that denial.

For the ultrarich, it was natural to downplay the Warming and the global consequences of their greed. In those days, the power of corporate propaganda had reached its zenith, and the dogma of consumption and growth was everywhere in the media. The idle rich had become "job creators," corporations had the rights of humans and humans were taught to be "brands."

And the Warming? Well, the corporate powers told us, in the post-COVID recession, there simply wasn't enough money for radical action.

But the World Strike changed everything.

Sunday, June 15

I should tell you a bit more about why I started writing these words.

Early in May, Dr. Leah messaged that we should schedule an in-person. I was surprised; like any septuagenarian, I keep a close eye on my dashboard and saw nothing to worry about. Every two months Dr. Leah sees me in the diagnostic booth at the New Williamsburg wellness center for a checkup. As far as I knew, I was a reasonably healthy elder.

So it was with some trepidation that, a week before 350 Day, I traveled to her office, in a walkable called Cressfield, about fifty kilometers west of Columbus.

Transport assigned me a public shuttle into Columbus and then a semi-private out to the Cressfield commons. I had a nice chat with a young couple, on their way to a birth center, sweetly excited to be starting gametogenesis. Of course, I told them all about you. Once we arrived in the town center I was booked for a cart; I'm a bit old to be assigned a scooter. But the day was beautiful and I decided to walk.

The village is set in reclaimed agricultural land, stands of trees and long sloping meadows, bordered with purple cress and wild geraniums, just then coming into bloom. Cressfield is small compared to your hometown—perhaps five thousand people in all, a typical second-generation walkable. New Williamsburg is old, built in the early 2030s, and like several of the early walkables it grew to nearly fifty thousand, simply because there were so many climate migrants and refugees back then.

Dr. Leah is in her fifties, quite lively, with a smart sense of humor. I sat and after a bit of small talk, she finally said, "It's about your Double."

Here's something you probably won't learn from Tutor: Humans weren't the first to have Doubles. Digital twins started way back when I was your age, as a maintenance technique for complex machines like jet engines or wind turbines. Smart sensors on the machines continually uploaded data about running time, temperatures, and mechanical data like vibrations or friction.

All that information went into the cloud to create a perfect, constantly updated software model of the real object, along with similar data from thousands of engines or turbines around the world. An analytic AI could then make predictions about potential failures. Even in the early century, a jet engine in flight could radio ahead to the next airport, requesting a replacement for a part that was projected to wear out in the next 50 hours.

You've had a Double since before you were born, starting with your geneprint. Your mother Sofia wore the usual prenatal sensors, so by the time you emerged squalling, there was already an infant Luca software model. Since then, your visits to the diagnostic booth and your in-persons have been added, as well as the data from the tiny mediloop on your wrist. So all the little shocks of childhood also shape your Double, whether a fall on the playground or an unpredicted allergy attack.

Gen Zs didn't get Doubles until we were in our thirties or forties, so our models lack quite a bit of early information. Doubles are only as good as their datasets, so the predictive function is fuzzier for Zs.

Even so, my Double saved my life when I was 60; it signaled an aortal wall weakness that would have caused an aneurysm and stroke within a few years. Dr. Leah sent me to a surgeon who injected a nanostent that resurfaced the interior of the aorta with stem cells. I came back in the next day, she triggered autodissolve on the stent, and announced that I was good for at least another 60 years. Not that I can imagine myself as a spry 120-year-old, but it was a nice thought.

On my visit three weeks ago, Dr. Leah said that my Double was once again sending an alert.

She immediately reassured me that we shouldn't worry too much. It was combining my readings with the Doubles of millions of others my age, all of us with limited early data, then cross-checking that with known diagnoses and outcomes and a dozen other strands of environmental and social input.

I knew all that, but waited patiently for her to get to the point.

"A lot of moving pieces," she said, "but there are trend lines that suggest a potential neurologic issue."

I was shocked. "What 'neurologic issue'?"

"Well, that's the difficult part. The AI is picking up something odd but has no firm diagnosis and can't fully explain its reasoning."

After forty years of repairing bots, I knew exactly what she was talking about.

Any AI whose function has real-world consequences is legally required to explain its reasoning. There's an even stricter standard for medical AIs. But the law also allows for "algorithmic intuition" as long as it is clearly labeled.

Algorithmic intuition is when a prediction is based on so much data, with connections so tenuous and complex, that the system can't explain the reasoning process in a way humans can understand. It's the AI version of a human hunch and, like our own intuition, can be very valuable. Other times, algorithmic intuition is a dead end. (Although Dr. Leah probably wouldn't use that exact phrase with a patient.)

These nebulous warnings are more common for Gen Z because our Doubles launched later in life, so we have generated limited datasets.

"Well," she said during that visit, as the breeze ruffled new green leaves outside the examining room windows, "you don't report symptoms, and your last month of balance and gait data are entirely normal. Keep taking take your neuroceuticals, regular mental and physical exercise. You know the routine."

Dr. Leah upgraded my mobility sensors and added language tracking as an input. My Double will begin monitoring my speech and writing, certain to notice slippage well before any humans might.

"Almost half the time," Dr. Leah told me as I was leaving that day, "algorithmic intuitions turn out to be erroneous. That's why they're sent straight to the physician rather than showing up on your dashboard."

"Well, that's reassuring," I said. "Almost half the time."

I departed with some cheerful inanities, but inside, all the way back to New Williamsburg, I felt something deeply ominous, my chest tight, as if I couldn't fully breath.

It was like those first hard, dark years after your grandmother Marianna died. In fact, had I heard this news back then, I might have told Dr. Leah, "Well, that's life. And how senile do I have to be before I can apply for Release and upholding?"

Now, however, there is more in my life. You, for example.

PERFECT WEATHER FOR AN AWAKENING

What finally broke the denial about the planet's fate wasn't "climate"—that was always too grand a timescale to figure into the tiny flicker of a human life. But *weather*—ah, there's something we perceive on the deepest, most primeval level. In the ancestral environment, the variability of weather meant life or death. When you think about it, all of our rituals and holidays were originally tied to weather. And weather triggered the Strike, beginning with three awful months in mid-2028.

For years earlier, researchers had warned about changes in ocean currents. By 2028, the ancient Atlantic current, buffeted by melting freshwater from the Arctic and Antarctic, was so unstable that all five of the major ocean gyres— north and south Atlantic and Pacific, plus the Indian Ocean—also became erratic. Oceans cover 70% of the Earth's surface; our liquid planet had turned against its most overbearing species.

Hurricane Belinda, the first Category 6 storm in this hemisphere, hit Miami nearly dead-on. Belinda devastated the city and surroundings so entirely that six months later Florida became the first US state to go bankrupt. (Florida was self-insured, since insurers had abandoned the market, but state bankruptcy was unconstitutional. The litigation on Florida lasted a decade and reached the Supreme Court.)

After Miami, Belinda turned north and hit New York City, wreaking the havoc that a few years later I would help repair, as one of the first generation of UniServ enlistees.

For the second year in a row, the hajj pilgrimage to Mecca was cancelled—even at night local temperatures often didn't drop below 110 and there was simply no way to keep two million humans alive. Australia suffered its worst flooding in recorded history—far worse than the "once-in-a-century" deluge of 2019. This time the damage was exacerbated by years of uncontrolled forest fires.

A massive permafrost collapse beneath an oil camp in Siberia killed over one hundred workers—crushed by the building, then drowned in a quicksand of liquefied tundra. At the same time Moscow restricted outdoor activity due to the choking smoke from enormous forest fires many hundreds of kilometers away. London declared a municipal heat emergency that shut down the city for five days; electricity usage was limited to fans and air-conditioning—and this was only three months after the city suffered its coldest winter day since the Little Ice Age of 1795. China instituted strict water rationing over most of the northeast; the Party sent thousands of "water cheats" to prison and work camps.

Of course, dozens of less-noted disasters occurred during the same three months; crop failures, atmospheric rivers, heat domes, firenados, derechos, disease outbreaks, EF5 tornado supercells, cyclonic bombs, and so-called blitzkrieg boomers, thunderstorms so sudden and fierce they could kill. And many smaller, more remote tragedies now lost to history.

Finally, there was the wind. To me, it seemed as if the wind changed after COVID, as if the planet's lungs had been damaged. But of course, it was really the Warming.

By the late 2020s, the wind blew nearly constantly, everywhere on the planet, changing directions unpredictably. It seemed as if the atmosphere could no longer make itself comfortable and was rushing back and forth, from one spot to another, trying to find some natural repose.

The air never rested: Even when the temperature and rainfall seemed normal, there was still the wind, a constant reminder to everyone on the planet that all was not well; a subtle, permeating sense of unease.

Some speculate that the ever-present wind was a shared experience, a global stimulus that galvanized the planet's emerging consciousness. Perhaps so; there is much we don't understand about the emergence of Nous. But the wind did fill the internet with endless streams of mutual commiseration, from San Diego to Santiago, from Berlin to Bengaluru. It was the one symptom of the Warming that was constantly shared by all.

THE IMPOSSIBLE STRIKE

The World Strike of 2029 was like nothing the planet had ever seen. Of course, "world strikes" over the Warming had already been happening for well over a decade—since I was in elementary school—but there was never the truly systematic global shutdown that might make a real impact.

And by then, there was more driving the Strike than simply climate. A long-term effect of the early century COVID pandemic, besides lingering medical conditions, was the deeper radicalization of the young. The pandemic had made global inequality far more severe, and the influence of the corporate powers and ultrarich was omnipresent.

Formal planning had started a year earlier. The Strike was called for April 22—a holiday then called "Earth Day." Dozens of countries had made Earth Day a national holiday in the mid-2020s—a small bone to toss to those noisy environmentalists. Thus many workers were already off for the day and simply never returned to the job.

Essential services such as healthcare, food, water, utilities remained. But across the developed world, and much of the developing, airplanes were grounded, mass transit closed, all non-essential retail shut, cinemas dark, streaming entertainment offline. Two-thirds of workers left their jobs. The robots in the vast e-tail warehouses went on standby as their human supervisors stayed home. Financial services limped along on emergency backup plans. Small businesses owners worldwide were not specifically targeted. The intent of the strike was to cripple the corporate powers and, by extension, the ultrarich.

Even in China, relatively isolated from the world on its insular national network, labor stoppages began to spread, and the Party, after four ominous days of silence, endorsed the Strike. Cynics argue that the Chinese acquiescence was a shrewd business move, given that nation's lead in renewable and sustainable technologies. And indeed the subsequent decades made China the richest country on the planet—although certainly not the happiest.

While people of all ages ultimately joined in, a majority of the early strikers were under thirty-five. I was in my first year at City College in New York. I worked with the CCNY planning committee for three months, recruiting students for various strike duties. Then I joined community organizers to distribute food; it was similar, older organizers said, to the mutual aid systems set up during the COVID crisis, when I was still a kid.

Thanks to the Warming, the April weather was moderate in New York City, so thousands of us slept in parks. The mayor joined the strikers in Zuccotti Park, which was then known for a much earlier (and prophetic) protest called "Occupy Wall Street." She announced that there would be no police activity unless strikers became violent or posed a threat to public safety. There was very little.

The goal was simply to stop the business of the planet. There were strikers in at least 70 different countries, and it was a similar story abroad: peaceful protests, surprisingly little violence, and largely sympathetic police forces. Much of local law enforcement had either suffered Warming damage themselves or had been deployed in disaster relief operations. Most remarkably, a half-dozen local military conflicts, mostly in Africa and Southeast Asia, announced "climate truces," just like the Christmas Truce on the front-lines in World War I.

However, the biggest and most effective Strike action was deployed at the end of the first day: The entire internet, across the planet, began to slow down.

It didn't stop completely. We strikers needed the internet to coordinate actions. But by prior plan, all of the Strike communication was done as simple text—no streaming, no audio, no video, no large files to upload and download. We used a new messaging app called Hansen, after one of the early climate scientists. Hansen had been launched three months earlier as a "low-carbon" alternative to existing messaging services, with its ultimate purpose undisclosed.

Prior to the Strike, thousands of young IT workers from around the world used an encrypted chat room to plan the digital slowdown: from Google to IBM, the New York Stock Exchange to a dozen global banks, Cambridge and Tsinghua to Stanford and the Technische Universitat Berlin—the list went on and on. It even included younger members of the Internet Engineering Task Force, the international group in charge of maintaining and improving the Web. Occasionally bits of their work would become public but it was easily explained as a volunteer task force to identify and prevent potential network weaknesses.

The global internet slowdown was a monumental collective hack, now the stuff of programming legend and a half dozen historical docs. The details were complex: coordinated teamwork between tens of thousands of IT departments and server farms in dozens of countries. The goal was to throttle the bandwidth on the global internet so that it became useless for large corporations and the financial sector.

World financial markets closed. International business slowed to a tenth of the pre-strike volumes. Banks shut down their ATM networks; the bank branches that still had human tellers were swamped with customers seeking cash.

But cash wasn't always necessary. Most of the basics of life were provided by volunteers or barter, and several regional grocery chains donated food. Funds had been crowd-sourced over the previous months should cash prove necessary. Many landlords promised to delay rent payments; smaller banks temporarily halted late fees on mortgage and loan payments. Much of what had been learned about community resilience during COVID turned out to be very helpful in the Strike.

Strike leaders arose on each continent—often well-known activists or social reformers, sometimes elected officials, a few influencers. But there was no truly international figure of authority. Much of Gen Z had come to mistrust charismatic, one-person leadership ever since the disastrous rise of the nationalist strongmen in the early century, whose "populist" policies in reality rarely benefited anyone under 30. And we'd seen too many leaders of our own generation torn to pieces by uncontrolled social media.

Perhaps solitary authority figures worked when the person with the loudest voice commanded the public space—cave, hut, village square—but with the Internet many voices could be heard. The difficulty, on the Internet, of course, had always been sorting all those voices out and determining the collective will.

But that was evolving as well.

The IT volunteers who engineered the slowdown and built the Hansen messaging system also adapted an AI market research agent used by the corporate powers. The AI was capable of reading millions of posts and synthesizing a general group opinion. It had previously been used to harvest consumer sentiment on weighty matters like dishwashing detergent or dog food. But it clearly had potential for higher purposes.

The volunteers added a voting option and gave it a goofy codename, Votetron, which, like many codenames, stuck. (Votetron was just the beginning of the rapid evolution of the commercial Internet in the 2030s and 2040s—and, some say, an element in the emergence of Nous.)

There was argument as to whether this approach to voting unfairly disenfranchised those without connection to the Internet. And perhaps it did. But there was a planet to save.

A team of ten representatives from around the world had been chosen to be the negotiating voice of the Strikers—the Board. Some reps were already famous; others had been nominated by the planet's leading environmental NGOs. The representatives pledged to remain true to the group opinion as generated daily by Votetron.

Historians now agree: the entire Strike governance was an ad hoc, exceedingly complicated, technically perilous, ridiculously fragile and borderline insane way to run an organization.

Yet somehow it worked.

JULY 2084

Monday, July 3

I'm taking a break. I'm incredibly slow at writing, and I've never tried something quite so ambitious as these essays. Some afternoons I develop a mild headache, which of course makes me worry about the warning from my Double. So today I spent a lazy afternoon on the roof of my apartment building.

Although I've lived in New Williamsburg for half a century, I still enjoy simply gazing over the town; down below, the wide plaza and its seasonal gardens, then the wellness center with the corny Wartime mural, and finally in the distance the gently-inclined gray roofs of the single-family section, where Marianna and I raised your father.

The original ugly solar roofs we had in the 2030s have long since been replaced with materials both more efficient and more esthetically pleasing. And the tree corridors around the walking and transport paths are now mature, offering deep cool shade in the hot Ohio summers.

These days, whenever I walk or bike to your parents' house, I can't help but remember those same paths, lined with slim saplings, on August afternoons fifty years ago, when I'd sweat through my shirt on the way to work.

After your grandmother Marianna's accident, your father and I moved to this townhouse on the plaza. Walkables make changing homes easier; you own the structure but the land is on a fifty-year lease from the New Williamsburg housing cooperative. Since shelter is a constitutional right, there are sliding scales for rent and purchase.

In the early century, if your parents didn't own a house, you probably weren't going to either. In cities like New York, the government had given up on low-cost housing; in a typical shareholder-value transaction, developers were given free rein to build whatever they wanted, as long as they put in a few "affordable" units that were nonetheless still priced for what remained of the middle class.

If you had told me, when I was a teenager in Brooklyn, that I'd spend most of my life in a small Midwestern town, I probably would have said: "Are you high?"

Yet here I am. Tonight my friend Mena is coming for dinner and then we'll watch a live concert in New York. It's from Carnegie Hall, piano concertos by Adams and Glass, two classical composers we enjoy. Mena and I have been friends for fifteen years now; we have grown close, despite our age and educational difference. At least I think so. Sometimes Mena is a bit of a mystery.

Anyway, I've loved watching this walkable start from almost nothing and become the enfolding community it is now. I am satisfied; sometimes I almost feel I've seen enough, as if, for me, the show is winding down. For you, of course, it is only beginning.

And so there is much more I need to tell you. Back to work...

THE CLIMATE DEMAND

On the second day, after the impact of the Strike and the slowdown became clear to world leaders, the Board put forward the Climate Demand: the planet's governments and the 500 largest corporate powers must pledge to reduce carbon dioxide output to zero by 2040 and increase carbon removal from the atmosphere to twenty billion tons a year.

Each government would clearly lay out the milestones it promised; if a milestone slipped, there would be either a national, regional, or world strike, accompanied by total economic sanctions by the cooperating nations. Additional money would go to disaster aid, relocating climate refugees, and building infrastructure resilience. Rich countries would contribute to a Climate Reparations and Justice fund that would assist poorer nations in recovery, resilience and carbon goals.

Little of the Climate Demand required invention—most of those measures had already been included in one or another international or regional agreement whose goals quietly slipped away. This time, however, all would be administered by a new organization, the United Nations Climate Authority, with full authority to call for economic sanctions.

The Climate Demand also banned "geoengineering." That was the idea of reversing the Warming by blasting a million tons of some substance into the upper atmosphere to filter the sun's rays.

Some of the biggest corporate powers had been promoting geoengineering as a solution. It would be a profitable business for them, and might also stifle the demands for carbon reduction thus giving the corporations more time to cash in their remaining fossil fuel deposits. The Board made it clear that the geoengineering ban was not negotiable: "We have done enough damage to our planet without further violent tinkering."

And there was one other very important clause: by 2034, 30% of every country's military budget would be reassigned to mitigation, recovery and decarbonization, to rise to 50% by 2037. The Demand put it simply: "Defense budgets should be spent on the true enemy, not on geopolitical conflicts created to defend corporate interests."

Those were the terms. The Board had been given authority to negotiate details, such as the exact timing of the defense budget shifts. But without agreement by the world's regional security and trade bodies, plus the largest global corporate powers, the Strike would continue.

The corporations of the planet had never faced such an uprising. How to turn back this tidal force of humanity?

Many of the most devoted defenders of corporate values were now elderly; by contrast, in 2029, nearly 25% of local politicians were under 40. And even the most successful tool of corporate control—propaganda—was muted by the Strike.

Right-wing news agencies went dark as their young technical staff walked out. Some of the right-wing commentators, portly white men, gaunt blond women, remained in the studios to sputter outrage, but to little impact. There were few young technicians behind the cameras or minding the microphones or tending the servers, and precious little bandwidth available to pump out malinformation.

All eyes were initially on the United States, still one of the world's most powerful defenders of fossil energy despite government protestations to the contrary. In 2029 it was fortunate that the US had a female president in her second term, less beholden to fossil fuel interests and open to cooperation and social good. After a long 48 hours, the US issued a call for an emergency UN session to discuss the settlement terms, and it was clear which way the tide was moving.

The Strike lasted eighteen days. On the nineteenth, Votetron determined that a majority of strikers were willing to accept the UN's Global Plan for Climate Justice, which included, in some form, all of the Strike demands.

The Global Plan also included new ideas for implementing this vast task, such as compulsory two-year national service for eighteen-year-olds—"Serving People and Planet"—a tradition which continues to this day.

It was clear from the outset that decarbonizing the planet would cost trillions. Everyone would need to contribute—money, time, or both. And the vast fortunes of the ultrarich, those thousands of billionaires and countless three-digit millionaires, were the most valuable resource in the world. The ultrarich had stashed enormous amounts of wealth into their digital hidey-holes. Those who had profited most should also pay to repair the damage.

After the Strike, most nations instituted new taxes on the holdings of the ultrarich and the corporate powers. No one was beheaded, but many of the rich went to prison for various flavors of tax fraud and money laundering. Early century governments had often punished financial crimes with monetary wrist slaps. Now, hoarding wealth was an attack on the survival of the planet and human life, and in some countries was punished as severely as attempted murder.

One question was much debated in the aftermath of the Strike: should the Deniers of the early century be tried for crimes against humanity? After all, it was clear that the corporate powers and the ultrarich had known for decades that the Warming was inevitable and did their best to deceive the world.

And even *after* they began to profess their commitment to reducing carbon in the early century, they nonetheless drilled for new oil and ordered their governments to continue giving fossil fuels an economic edge. And then there were the collaborators: the writers, scholars, and politicians rewarded for defending the interests of the corporate powers. The words and deeds of the propagandists also cost lives.

Trials of prominent Deniers did occur in some areas—Scandinavia, South America, China. China even held a handful of executions; well into mid-century, Chinese leaders still favored the occasional salutary execution. But the global consensus was that show trials for Deniers would be a distraction that ultimately solved no real problem.

And trials might imply that only certain individuals were responsible for the Warming, while in fact we were almost all complicit in our daily choices. Thus we were all called upon, in various ways, to begin repairing the planet.

FAMILY HISTORY: NEW YORK CITY 2030

Both your American great-grandparents were excellent teachers, but I was never the best student. Naming me after a famous printer of early books didn't help my reading skills.

I was probably somewhere in the middle of the dyslexia spectrum, not enough to qualify for special help in school—although my parents did pay for a few years of a private tutor, a difficult financial stretch for two public school teachers in New York City. It was decades before I learned to enjoy reading and writing, thanks to Tutor Alice.

The feeling that I was a disappointment to my parents never really left me. In an attempt to lessen that feeling, I started college. Back then it was considered absolutely essential, although the actual vocational value of most college degrees was often low. It was unclear exactly what we were supposed to do with some of the subjects we studied, since in the early century good jobs had more to do with family connections and luck than possessing a diploma. I dropped out after my first year at City College, and never did earn a degree.

But I had a much better alternative, as did millions of my generation.

Like so many parts of the Climate Demand, the notion of national service already existed in the early century. Only now, the entire planet needed service. In the months following the Strike, the US and dozens of other nations passed Universal Service Acts. In the US, every citizen was required to register for UniServ at age eighteen, and spend two years serving in the War on the Warming.

You could still volunteer for the military, but as funding shifted to the War, the interesting opportunities for training and education were found in UniServ. In 2072, right after your father's service in Sicily, the requirement for UniServ was reduced to one year, so that's likely what you'll serve when you grow up.

Instead of starting my sophomore year at CCNY, I volunteered for UniServ in September 2029, the first deployment. You could get a four-year college deferment, but more than half my classmates volunteered after freshman year. (A further deferment was available for graduate school, but only for healthcare or sci/tech studies.)

The big decarbonization projects took time to start up, so in the 2030s the emphasis was disaster relief: assisting areas stricken by floods, fires, tidal surges, mudslides, cyclones, tornadoes, hurricanes, drought and derechos. Millions of young people around the world gained skills in emergency medicine, food and water distribution, infrastructure repair, even psychological counseling.

UniServ also helped with "prevention and mitigation." This was the science and craft of rebuilding homes and cities, seaports and highways, energy and communications infrastructure, to withstand the extreme weather onslaughts that were inevitable for decades to come. (Much of that knowledge came from insurance companies, which started preparing for the crisis far earlier than did public officials. Out of pure self-interest, the companies funded research on how to construct buildings they could afford to insure.)

For the first six months, I was deployed for salvage and fortification work on Staten Island and in the new Brooklyn tidal zones. UniServ started up so quickly that at first there were not even places to house recruits, so only New York City residents from climate-safe neighborhoods were assigned to the work. At CCNY we were allowed to stay in the dorms for our first year of service. Very few kids were arriving to take our places as first year students: You could volunteer right after high school and go into training, as long as you were eighteen by the time your active duty started.

UniServ also had an enormous social impact. Many deep friendships, marriages, partnerships came out of the struggles of the 2030s and 2040s.

In fact, that's how I met your grandmother. But that was later.

THE INTERNET

The internet accelerated it all—initially, the bad parts. The problem, we now know, was not the network itself; ultimately the network would save our species. The problem was the "business model."

A bit of obscure history. The internet was born in grand innocence—on the San Francisco mid-peninsula, in the idealistic glow of my favorite decades, the 1960s and 1970s, the era of "peace and love."

Thus, the technology was initially bathed in optimistic countercultural themes. Activists set up storefronts where anyone could use a free computer. Hardware-makers had whimsical names, like Kentucky Fried Computers, or Apple. An influential writer of rock songs published "A Declaration of the Independence of Cyberspace."

Good intentions at the start, but trouble was ahead. This tiny, fragile seed of the global mind happened to germinate in the United States, a nation that in the 1980s adopted "shareholder value" as the fundamental measure of social worth.

The corporate powers proceeded to create an unregulated and cutthroat society. By the early 21st century, even the inhabitants of rich nations such as the United States desperately scrambled for commercial advantage in a manner not much evolved from the 19th century. As hard as it is to believe, getting seriously ill, or losing a job, could plummet one into poverty in a matter of months. Even my well-born high school classmates competed ruthlessly to go to "elite universities," lest they be left on the roadside.

As the Internet moved into wider public use in the early 1990s, it became measured by its "profitability," and from this unhappy start flowed many ills. By the early 21st century, everything on the internet, from access to privacy to data, was for sale, and valued only in financial terms. It was the perfect recipe for an inhumane machine.

Or more accurately, a deeply troubled *mind*: the internet of those days was a brain in spasm, a writhing digital id, a tortured unconscious swept by hallucinations and seizures and awful visions, and disordered behavior with names like "troll" or "spoof" or "flame."

One highly contagious hallucinatory disease of the early internet was conspiracy delusion. (There's a great history doc about this disease called *The Age of QAnon*.)

The rise of conspiracy delusion was much like the origin of the Black Death in the Middle Ages. Bubonic plague had long existed in nature, but it was the invention of crowded cities that made it widely lethal. Similarly, conspiracy theories had always existed, a misguided byproduct of the human drive to assemble disparate facts into stories. The early internet, where information was valued only by the attention it attracted, turned this drive into a pandemic. One reason COVID deaths were high in the United States was due to co-infection with conspiracy delusion.

While conspiracy delusion remained a problem throughout the 2020s, it diminished as the scale and undeniability of the Warming became obvious. Another big help was the decline of anonymity, but that's a separate essay. The dwindling of this delusion may have also been evidence that our species' tormented virtual mind was already being healed by the emergence of Nous, although it would be several more decades before we even had a name for it.

Sometimes I wonder: what if the internet had been born and nurtured in one of the European social democracies, rather than the US, and had thus been shaped by different values?

At the outset it might have been a kinder, more humane network. But without the implacable and unchecked greed of the American corporate powers, the internet never would have evolved quickly enough to help turn back the Warming. And I shudder to think what kind of world you would now inherit.

Friday, July 14

I worked at your PreK yesterday; your father is traveling so I covered his shift. I spent my three hours in the kitchen, running the vegetable prep for your afternoon snack. Not too complicated: unload the bins from the delivery bot and attach them to the prepper. Even when out of season, the produce is very fresh: It comes from the same vertical farm I use for home delivery, about four kilometers outside of town.

There were a half-dozen parents at the co-op, either working in the kitchen, or setting out play materials, while the professional caregivers looked after you and your friends.

Co-ops were rare when I was young, but you will consider them normal. The co-op movement grew very quickly after the World Strike—it was an easy and immediate way for people to disentangle important parts of our lives from the corporate powers.

The Internet made organizing cooperatives easy. The software originally came from the so-called "sharing economy" startups of the early century, with names like Uber and AirBnb, which ironically had little to do with sharing. The early "sharing economy" was actually about replacing full-time employees in areas like transportation and hospitality with gig workers.

By the end of the 2040s, co-ops covered most of the fundamental life activities: early childcare, tool sharing, food, meal prep and delivery. They require membership, and each member must work, usually four to six hours a month. For those who don't have the time or inclination to work cooperatively, there are always private caregivers, schools, and food distributors; the for-profits are more expensive and certainly far less personal.

People love to complain about their co-op jobs. For decades, comedy series based on crazy work shifts were standard middlebrow fare. But that's part of being human in society, and few would actually quit.

In fact, cooperators always ask: what else would you do with the leisure hours that full automation and Living Income has given us? The opportunity to spend a few hours in life activities can be more satisfying than a hobby. For parents, the involvement in childcare, even just working in the kitchen or stocking supplies, is fulfilling and reassuring. (And if parents like the work, they can use their education credits for professional training. The skills for raising children aren't automatically included with the birth certificate.)

After your grandmother died, I was no longer so much a cooperator myself, but I didn't mind filling in on your parents' shifts once in a while—after all, it gave me a chance to stop in and see my best and only grandchild.

And watching the co-op activity always cheers me up. When I was young, for much of my generation, childcare was very different. There was a stark division between working and caregiving parents—it seemed you had to be one or the other. To afford our apartment in Brooklyn, both my parents worked as teachers; my mother was back to school a month after my birth, and I had a series of "nannies."

Childcare labor was haphazardly distributed among for-profits and gig workers paid minimum wage or less. The system was not a natural way of life; the devaluation of basic life support activities was another corrosive artifact of "shareholder value." Parents caring for children didn't make any money for the corporate powers. In particular, women could not afford to leave the workplace even briefly; in the corporate world, regardless of company "policy," children were perceived to compromise the dollar value of women's labor.

Back then, raising a child was expensive in many ways. As a result, couples often waited until their late 30s or early 40s to have children. Then, in the mid-2030s the US instituted universal childcare and PreK. Now, childcare and education are two of the larger sectors of our working economy.

Today, even with much longer lifespans, couples tend to start families at a younger age than when I was a child. Your mother was 27 and your father 30 when you were born. The co-op always reminds me that it's good to have the energy of youth while raising children.

* * *

Today, as I was leaving, I paused to watch you, playing with a half-dozen other kids in a big sunlit atrium overlooking a hillside of white oaks, newly leafing, intensely green.

You've just reached the age when you will be guided into virtuality. Until now, you have been exploring the richness and complexity of the physical world. The analog—air, soil, the tactile—is our species' real home, even though many adults may ultimately choose to spend much of their time in the virtual. But we always remember where we came from.

We now know how important it is to introduce the young human mind to the virtual world in gentle stages, with much coaching and practice. Virtual life is a skill; would we toss a two-year-old into a deep swimming pool and expect the child to paddle happily away?

Of course, there's no way to isolate a toddler from the virtual world; screens, images, bots, active walls are everywhere. But solitary time in the virtual world is ideally limited to no more than two hours a week. To park a three-year-old at the dinner table with a glowing screen as a pacifier—as was common practice in my youth—is today borderline child abuse.

Your first two years of childcare have been entirely analog, playing coordination and social games with the other children, or pushing dirt around in the community garden. You've practiced weaving with wooden dowels and thick yarn, you've helped cook simple meals, you've done all kinds of silly activities that are in fact precise exercises to develop spatial and social skills and dexterity while your neurons are still plastic.

Last fall, for example, your pod made bread out of acorns from the white oaks just outside your care room. You kids used stone tools, as the Shawnee once did, but most of the flour was actually made in the kitchen by parents wielding primitive food processors. (No one makes an acorn bot.) Your mother spent an entire work shift cracking acorns and then leaching the flour. Talk about tedious; I'm glad I wasn't filling in that day.

Today I watched you briefly. You were totally engrossed in some project that involved building a model of the solar system out of wire and clay.

Soon you'll start bot training, easy playful tasks for the very young and a gentle transition into virtuality. You'll train soft bots to race each other around obstacle courses, or build wind turbine platforms out of smart blocks, or teach drones to fly in formation like geese, or flock and whirl like pigeons. These exercises will teach you to use the virtual world to control the physical, and the logical concepts behind algorithmic thought.

I doubt you'll follow in my vocational footsteps; you may grow up never to program another bot. But you will always have the language of algorithm in your life. As with learning any language, the sooner your neurons are shaped to the grammar, the more natural your understanding will be.

VIRTUALITY

When I was young, in the early 2020s, I used to joke that I was born in the wrong century. I would have loved to be alive in the 1960s; I liked the idea of an era more analog than my own. I suppose that's another reason your father ended up as Dylan. Life then was about being present, touching, feeling, tactility, the here-and-now. No one even *knew* about the virtual world, so no one missed it. It would be another twenty years before the term "cyberspace" even existed.

Now, of course, I feel much differently. The virtual world helped save our species from extinction. And the unexpected emergence of Nous has made the human a better creature. We know that virtuality is a major step forward in human evolution, perhaps the most important since the opposable thumb. But it did not seem so in the early 2020s.

As you are gradually introduced to virtuality in the next few years, you will share the virtual world with your parents, just as you do the physical world. But in the first few decades of the 21st century, the onset of virtual life was so rapid that it separated even older children from their younger siblings in behavior. The Millennial woman of twenty seven was often appalled by the online habits of her Gen Z sister of seventeen.

We of Gen Z—I am among the youngest of that generation—were the first to enter the virtual world from birth. But our parents and teachers lacked experience in the virtual realm and had little useful advice to offer, beyond dire warnings. I suppose evolution can be difficult for parents. Hundreds of millions of years ago, when the first fish hauled themselves from the primordial sea onto solid land, their fish parents probably shouted: "Don't go there! It's too dangerous!"

In my teens, I had mixed feelings about this amorphous digital foundling called the Internet. And I was hardly alone. In its early form the network was abused and misused and degraded on all sides, by the autocrats and the greedy, the ill-spirited and ignorant. It divided society, compromised mental health. Experts taught classes and wrote books about "getting off" the Internet; in some countries young people were interned in camps for "addiction." Our species overdosed on the first heady fumes of virtual life. It is amazing that Nous survived at all.

When you begin studying with Tutor, you will see all the lamentable stereotypes of the 2020s: a zombified population shuffling from place to place, numbly focused on a tiny glass rectangle clutched in hand. Or "selfie" addiction, whose sufferers could never, ever upload enough of their images to the cloud. The video from the early century makes it appear that we were all clumsy, with atrocious manners—tumbling off curbs, walking into traffic (potentially fatal in the era of freehand driving), ignoring the people around us.

And much of that is true—I was often guilty of similar actions. I grew up with all the same digital trinkets that now provoke teary nostalgia among elders: Fortnite skins, Snapchat streaks, Telegram stickers, TikTok challenges...

(OK, enough. Luca, I'm sure your eyes are glazing over. When I was young, if Baby Boomers grew tiresome, we would just shrug and say "OK Boomer." Now it's our turn, and I know perfectly well that bored young people sometimes call us Gen Zzzzzzz.)

But I could not have had a normal teenage life without such things; those were our public spaces. Unlike most of my friends, I was always a little shy on the socials, never quick and quippy and adept. So for the sake of public appearance, I tried to pride myself on being a touch retro, with what I felt was focused and present behavior. Yet dozens of times a day I found myself staring at a screen without quite knowing how it happened.

Someday you'll watch *I'm Right Here*, a nostalgic rom-com from 2065 or so. The story is set in the early century, in which the two lovelorn protagonists constantly miss reconnecting because of their awkward transitions from real to virtual. There's a scene where they actually lose their cloud connection, called "offline"; hilarious, although you won't understand that until you get a bit older. The period details are very accurate, and even the lead characters were generated from early century actors, Julia Roberts and Brad Pipp.

(Autofact prompts me with "Pitt." Actually, Pitt sounds right. I won't use autoparser but autofact is fine with me.

Who can remember everything? Certainly not me, at least recently.)

Even my aging generation looks back and laughs at those old images, compared to our ability now to move smoothly between the analog and the virtual. "To live with an eye in each," as you will be taught. In the early century we were very far from that ideal.

We were, instead, perennially distracted. Virtuality emerged faster than any other environmental change in history. Consider our early ancestors, 100,000 years ago in the Serengeti. Their sensory systems were trained to perceive a limited set of objects—food, water, threats, mates. If you suddenly dropped one of them into the middle of modern New York City, they would be perpetually distracted too.

Our transition into more graceful virtuality is partly due to better technology—iglasses, audio implants and bone conduction, active contacts, retinal projectors, and so on, devices to which we are so accustomed that they seem quite invisible. When we are in dualview, our eye pieces keep fragments of the digital floating in the air around us at all times, as do the active walls we live with, the live windows, the nooks and corners of our homes—everywhere we see bits of the virtual world woven into the real.

When you're older, you'll move quite naturally through notes or images from friends, tag clouds, personal reminders or inspirations, maps, information about objects or people near or distant in your eyeline. Except, of course when you visit an analog zone and switch off dualview. (At least, that's what we're supposed to do in an analog zone.)

When I was your age, however, we humans seemed destined for perpetual distraction. The virtual world became a compulsion. Although our initial contacts with the virtual world might have been negative—addictions, alienation, distraction, depression, youth suicide—we were unable to turn away, because in fact we were evolving. There was something in the virtual world we wanted very much.

FAMILY HISTORY:
NEW YORK CITY 2031

Manhattan sustained limited damage from Hurricane Belinda at the end of 2028 because there had already been much defensive work on the shorelines. The outer boroughs, however—Brooklyn, Staten Island, parts of Queens—were hit very hard, with severe destruction of thousands of homes and vast segments of power and water infrastructure in tatters. Worse, repairs had only just started when a late season tropical storm arrived. That storm, fueled by an atmospheric river, set a new historical record for City rainfall in a single day.

It was over a half-century ago, but I still recall the shock of seeing my first American climate refugees: people with almost nothing left, and no way to make themselves whole again. You can see those faces today, in the images from the Warming Arts Initiative, which employed thousands of artists to document the War.

WAI also created public artworks—murals, sculptures, soundscapes, active walls—to accompany new construction, everywhere from apartment buildings and flood barriers to the old carbon sequestration plants. In our town, the figures you see on the facade of the Wellness Center are supposed to be UniServ recruits hoisting a stretcher with a little planet Earth on it. Yes, corny, but sometimes that's how we were back then.

The first priority for UniServ in New York City was sheltering refugees. Along with the National Guard, we installed thousands of trailer homes in public parks, beside shopping malls, next to hospitals, even in the parking lot of a city jail. Often it was two families to a small trailer, and it wasn't clear when they'd be able to move on. We set up medical clinics, ran water lines, built little playgrounds for the kids. The "shelters" were essentially refugee camps for our own citizens.

All this, in what was then still the richest nation in the world. Families, young professionals, elderly lifelong residents—people who believed they would be kept safe—were all displaced, with no clear prospect on when, if ever, they would have their own homes again.

Early in the 2030s, UniServ began a new mission called "Managed Retreat." At that point at least thirty million Americans were living in coastal areas or flood zones where the future weather threat could not be mitigated. They could choose to remain, but neither private insurance nor government programs would still cover losses. Harsh, but inevitable.

These climate migrants were gradually relocated inland or to higher ground, often temporarily placed in rental housing. New walkable villages were constructed, away from the coasts, to permanently remove people from danger zones. The walkables became the model for new housing throughout the US; our town, New Williamsburg, was one of the first in the mid-2030s.

To simplify the startup of the relocation program, the Federal government reactivated a century-old agency called the Resettlement Administration, dating from the Dustbowl era in the 1930s. After a few years this became the Climate Security Administration, as it remains today.

When my UniServ squad wasn't assisting refugees, we cleared land in the outer boroughs. I still have nightmares about dragging away unending quantities of filthy pink fiberglass insulation, all entangled in twisted two-by-fours and electrical wiring. In Brooklyn, land once covered with neat rows of houses now ends abruptly with tall seaward levees that you can see all the way from Manhattan.

Funding for refugee and migrant resettlement was, ironically, more difficult in the United States than in many other nations. The Climate Demand had been very clear about the financial responsibilities of the rich nations for resettlement in the developing world. It was less specific about how the rich countries would deal with their own refugees.

In the years since COVID, our federal government remained in perpetual deep deficit. And so in the first year or so of the War, much of the relief money came from the charities of the corporate powers and the ultrarich. But even then, there was not enough to go around.

This led most of us on the frontlines to wonder why we were depending on the charitable impulses of the wealthy rather than the resources of a properly funded government. This only increased the political momentum for new corporate and wealth taxes, and by the mid-2030s we started to pull back the vast sums of money that the ultrarich had removed from society.

GREED

The early century was probably the best time in human history to be rich, and the United States was the best country in which to be so. Back then, most Americans loved the rich, since many still had the hallucinatory expectation that they might themselves be rich someday. (My generation was the first to awaken en masse from this delusion.) The corporate media glorified the yachts and penthouses, and studied the social feeds of the wealthy like religious texts. Business writers quoted the words of the ultrarich as if they were prophets.

Even the popular music I grew up on often celebrated wealth, with displays of physical money and gold and costly automobiles and other ostentatious symbols of consumption. And because American popular culture was so globally infectious (Americans would do anything for clicks!), that love for the rich began to infuse even countries that should have known better.

Now, a half century later, when students study economic history, their first question is often: *"Why were there billionaires in the first place?"*

Well, by the mid-2020s there were no real limits to the amount of money billionaires could amass. Once a family was rich, neither intelligence nor talent was needed to accrue additional wealth. Powered by financial networks, artificial intelligence and lax regulation, the ultrarich had created a global wealth-gathering system that suctioned up resources like a giant planetary vacubot.

As more labor was automated by AI and bots, the increased profits accrued solely to the owners of software and capital. Money attracted money, accelerating and snowballing so dramatically that as the end of the 2020s approached, already a half-dozen men and two women were trillionaires.

Yet in a matter of a few decades, the lives of the ultrarich went from objects of admiration and wonder to anger, derision—and now, understanding and pity.

There is a wonderful source document used with younger students called "Rich Kids of Instagram." You'll be shocked when you see it. It's very early-century, a primitive image scroll, but this gleeful display of money and automobiles and extreme leisure is horrifying for young people today. Bottles of costly champagne poured down a toilet! Private helicopters! Setting handfuls of paper cash ablaze! And this from young people not much older than the students themselves.

I remember when your father was seven or eight and came back from a session with Tutor quite upset. He'd seen "Rich Kids." I reminded him that these ugly, brutal images are many years old. Times were very different then, and these children were ill. Do not be so quick to judge. He thought about this for a moment and then blurted out:

"Wasn't this also when everyone had guns? Why didn't someone just *shoot* those kids?"

I explained that yes, there were many guns in the US then, and many different kinds of people were shot, but very rarely rich ones.

Years before the disease concept of greed emerged, the ultrarich were already losing their social cachet. One early trigger that Tutor may not teach was, of all things, a children's book, written by two young Norwegians in 2030, shortly after the Strike.

If We Shared used simple, colorful graphics to tally the trillions of dollars locked up across the planet in real estate and gold and airplanes and yachts and art vaults and the many other secret places where the ultrarich warehoused their wealth.

With equal simplicity, *If We Shared* then showed what could be done if that wealth was applied to human needs such as water, food, healthcare, shelter, and the repair of the planet.

"An absurdly misleading approach to a complex problem," said *The Wall Street Journal*, "and any adult who takes this seriously must themselves have the mind of a child."

But that simple children's book captured the global imagination, children and adults. It was as if the entire planet decided to read the same book at the same time. *If We Shared* was almost instantly translated into fifty-five languages, as well as a lively interactive version in both video and VR formats, and a vast online community. The twenty-something authors used their profits to launch the If We Shared Foundation, which continues even now to fund research into community and cooperation.

Why was *If We Shared* so influential? There wasn't a thought in it that hadn't been expressed repeatedly and more fluently during the preceding five centuries, yet that slim children's book helped reshape much of the planet's economy. Why were humans at that point finally able to hear? Was it the earliest collective spirit of Nous at work? We still don't know.

In the first years of the War, dozens of governments—all of the developed world and even the Russia oligarchy—instituted War taxes on their ultrarich. But even with much higher taxes, it was still a gradual decline for the ultrarich: they controlled so much state power around the world that it was never easy to enact new taxes. Slowly, however, the vast fortunes were reduced, whittling away at this new global aristocracy.

And it *was* an aristocracy: Just like historical aristocrats, the ultrarich intermarried, combining fortunes, living in grand castles guarded by private armies. They differed from the nobility of old only in that the ultrarich pledged fealty to the corporate powers rather than to the Church.

By the late 2030s, there was a definite stigma attached to the children of inherited wealth, although it was impolite to mention it. It wasn't their fault, of course, and heirs often strived far harder than the rest of us to distribute their wealth. For example: the early-century ultrarich loved to build enormous palaces, monstrosities with ten or fifteen bedrooms, equipped with all the features of a costly resort.

Many of the castles were ocean-front, and were ultimately abandoned to the rising tides. Those that survived were handed down to Gen-Z heirs and are now often co-op living residences, or art and craft retreats where sojourns can be funded with ed creds.

Today, to die with excessive wealth reflects a life poorly lived. One leaves one's children skills, values and a network of friends. These are true legacies.

Our language began to reflect new attitudes as well. Today, to be called a "consumer" is an insult. At least it's certainly nothing you should say to anyone, no matter how piqued you might be.

By contrast, when I was young, the word "consumer" was quite neutral. Gradually it fell into disfavor for its implication of consumption without reciprocation. The self-aggrandizement of, say, a costly handbag with a waiting list is largely incomprehensible to us now. Money spent on supporting craftsmanship and the arts, or building and enhancing public resources, is money admirably spent.

The biggest shift in our attitude toward extreme wealth came with the discovery that greed is a disease, triggered by a combination of heredity and environment. It is caused by a gene cluster (as are virtually all of the more interesting human traits) so genomic intervention is difficult.

When the cluster was identified in the early 2040s, the disease concept of greed launched strong debate. Most people then considered greed to be a failure of character or a personality flaw. But that opinion was no different than, say, the 19th century belief that alcoholism was a moral failing, or epilepsy a sign of mental derangement.

Other researchers attacked the science—how the condition of greed was defined, how its activity in an individual was measured. But the research was solid. And when the study was published, most of the developed world immediately plugged the cluster into their own geneprints to look for matches.

I did—who could resist? I read out at the very low end of the greed spectrum, not surprising considering that my ability and desire to acquire money has always been limited, at best. But others discovered that they had significant tendencies toward greed—and it usually fit the person. Therapy ensued for millions.

These days the greed cluster is not necessarily a red light for parents-to-be during zygote selection, since parts of the cluster are also loosely tied to socially beneficial traits such as thrift. If a child is known to have the cluster, then early VR therapy will almost always suppress pathologic greed.

More reassuring is that even untreated greed is seen only occasionally in modern society, because, for the susceptible, greed is triggered by *perceived* scarcity—by distorted perception rather than reality.

Starting in the 20th century, shareholder-value economies used the appearance of scarcity as a very efficient motivating tool. Even for the wealthiest there was always a scarcity of something: the most luxurious homes, the best schools, expensive automobiles. In every stratum of society, there was never quite enough to go around. Perceived scarcity, in short.

If you eliminate the fear of losing one's income, as we have with Living Income, and ensure that every citizen has physical and mental wellness, and that most people are not grossly dissimilar in actual wealth, the incidence of pathologic greed drops precipitously. When happiness and social worth are defined by human ties and meaningful work, the urge to hoard wealth rarely arises.

There are, of course, those unfortunates whose genetic predisposition to greed is so compulsive that it still emerges, even in polite society. When greed does surface in adults, it usually causes deep embarrassment and shame. Fortunately, a microdose of targeted mRNA inhibitor, once monthly, suppresses these unattractive urges.

CRIME

Along with the rich, crime is another early century remnant that is far less common than when I was young.

Violence has diminished substantially, beginning with guns.

Beginning in the mid-2030s, ID chips were required in all firearms, first in the more liberal "blue" states and then nationally; unless you were properly licensed and trained, the gun would not function. It also records the time and place of each discharge. This continues today, and disabling the chip disables the weapon.

The chips mean that in dualview you will always get a signal when a gun is nearby. Concealed weapons are a mysterious part of history: would you allow someone to carry, say, a concealed rattlesnake?

The explosive-charge guns you'll see in the old movies are rare and usually a hobby. Modern weapons used by law enforcement are non-lethal directed energy, meant to stun rather than kill.

(Now that I think about it, Luca, you may see an antique

gun when you visit your mother's family in Sicily. Your grandfather has an ancient gunpowder rifle he uses to thin the rabbit population around his vegetable garden. When your mother was growing up, she tried without luck to convince him to buy a small mammal stunner instead. But these days his vision has declined and the local bunnies are safe.)

Living Income and full employment have greatly reduced economic crimes like theft, fraud, and robbery. They still happen, of course, but now usually there is some underlying disorder that triggers the behavior.

And we're working on that. Early childhood education plus the presence of Tutor helps identify in-born antisocial tendencies, which can often be reoriented to the positive with VR therapy and human counselors. Major psychoses are usually detected in zygote scans, but even if undiscovered until childhood, are usually treatable.

And then there are the so-called "drug-related offenses." A range of crimes, from shoplifting and burglary to gang warfare, declined dramatically as recreational drugs were decriminalized in the early century. Locking people in prison because they used a certain drug will make little sense to you. It was as if addiction was a contagious disease and the afflicted required quarantining in isolated cells—as if we might have quelled the COVID pandemic by making the virus illegal.

That was, of course, very confused thinking. In retrospect there were three reasons people used recreational drugs. The first two were unfortunate: to numb unpleasant elements of life or due to addiction disorder. The third was positive: People *enjoyed* drugs, and there is nothing wrong with that.

During the 20th century, anti-drug scolds used to say "drugs are for people who can't handle reality." Well, exactly! Reality is relative. We all like to tweak or augment or entirely invent our realities from time to time. In analog times, drugs were the easiest way to do that.

Addiction is now known to be another gene cluster trait. These days, people who do carry the cluster usually don't manifest the disorder; escape from a harsh society is no longer a motivation. And if addiction does occur, it is readily treatable.

Finally, most modern recreational pharmaceuticals are designed to minimize addiction. Even THC, the loveliest of molecules in its natural state, has dozens of genetic and chemical tweaks to tune its effects.

But there is one category that persists: crimes of passion.

Jealousy is so deeply wired into our evolutionary engine that it is exceedingly difficult to mitigate. During your grandmother Marianna's time as a relationship counselor, separating love from jealousy was an issue that she often dealt with, even among her most committed virtual couples.

Evolutionary psychology explains the primeval quest for optimal genetic pairings and certainty of parenthood that fuels jealousy. That understanding, however, offers little respite for those suffering its torments. Like most human emotions, jealousy is composed of additional threads, like ego and power, which combine to create a singularly persistent emotion.

Over the past fifty years, the blending of analog and virtual relationships has created new degrees of jealousy. And unlike most psychological discomforts, jealousy can rarely be treated by AI counseling; Marianna used to joke that it was a lifetime employment guarantee for human counselors.

It's a bit theoretical for me these days. Mena and I have grown much closer in the last year or so, but we come and go in each other's lives quite naturally. I don't really feel any jealousy about Mena's other companions, and I'm quite sure she feels none about me. Although of course I've become such a solitary soul that there's really no one of whom to be jealous.

Our relationship is nothing like what I had with Marianna. Perhaps even with all the various options of coupling and uncoupling we have now, there's only one truly great love in each lifetime.

But I digress…

FAMILY HISTORY:
NEW YORK CITY 2032

During my first years in UniServ, I went to work every day on the subway or a ferry, which began carrying scores of young recruits in our government-issue boots and hard-hats, in addition to the usual commuters. In the old days, New Yorkers being New Yorkers, there might have been a bit of quiet grumbling among the commuters about how much space we took up. But this was a different time, and there was now a real sense that we were all in this together.

Many of the existing social divisions and conflicts were exacerbated by the Warming in the early century—income inequality, racism, nationalism. Now, perhaps, these wounds were starting, very slightly, to heal. I remember wondering if this is how it had been in World War II; a diverse and fractious population a bit more knitted together by fighting a common foe. WWII was a small start, but it was followed by several decades of social progress.

The War against the Warming would also lead, in time, to so much more: the reinvention of education, Work for

All, the diagnosis of greed, the Living Income Act, and of course the rise of Nous.

How could I have explained the sweep of the transformation ahead to my young self, back in 2030, going to work every day in the devastated Brooklyn tidal zones? Impossible. It would have seemed a dear, sweet fantasy.

I spent all of my initial two-year enlistment in New York City, for the first year working in the outer boroughs. Then, since I'd taken a few shop classes in high school (my favorite classes, actually), I was assigned to public housing rehabilitation. The goal was to use funding from the Climate Justice Initiative to improve the extreme weather resilience of the projects. But it was actually a fundamental rethinking of public housing. My division worked on two 30-story public housing towers: smart zero emission buildings designed as functioning high-rise "walkables," complete with urban farms and telepresence work centers.

UniServ mixed Americans of all classes, colors, genders and educational backgrounds. From the start, people of color were the majority in UniServ, as they were, for the first time in US history, in my generation.

By the mid-2030s, an increasing number of White children grew up naturally considering themselves a minority among other minorities. It was a profound psychological shift. Just as the Warming didn't end on the first 350 Day, that shift in the younger generation didn't immediately demolish systemic racism. But looking back, it was a turning point.

Since New York duty was still limited to local residents, I was definitely a minority in my squad, a skinny White kid from Park Slope working with East New York Blacks,

Latinx from the Bronx, a half-dozen Asians of various ethnicities. We had music, sports, and gaming in common, and that was a good beginning. Pretty soon we were giving dap like we all lived on the same block.

In the unified effort against the Warming, we started to build a new sense of national cohesion, and the importance of equity. That cohesion was amplified in subsequent years by steady social progress, along with the increasing mix of races and ethnicities in new families.

And of course, Luca, you are part of that. Anglo-Sicilian-Guatemalan...the girls are going to love you. (I know... eye-roll...*Nonno, you are a hopeless old genderist...*)

In 2084 we can hardly claim a society devoid of intolerance, but we are moving in the right direction. Perhaps in your lifetime we will finally classify the dark emotions of racism and intolerance the same way we now understand greed: as a mental disorder.

EARLY CENTURY POLITICS

When I was a kid, the United States elected a mentally ill man to be its president, one of the strangest American political events of this century. This was long before the Digital Voting amendment; back then, the centuries-old electoral system was deeply flawed. Even when a candidate received the most votes, they might not actually win.

If that's not enough to baffle students today, there's also the question of how a person so disordered was even allowed to be President. Now we can diagnose and usually mend the several forms of character disorder the President carried.

But the country was disordered as well. After four years of a chaotic regime that ended in physical violence against Congress, a traditional president was elected. He was a White male, loyal to the corporate powers, but also far saner and more humanistic.

The new president could do little to quell the turmoil. The Twenties were a vortex of hard historical forces, many worldwide.

Starting toward the end of the last century, the global

corporate powers began to abandon many Americans, particularly those in the middle of the country. Far cheaper labor and lower environmental standards could be found elsewhere on the planet. Income and education inequality grew so great in the United States that various groups—the wealthy, the urban poor, the underemployed in the countryside—seemed to be living in different nations. And briefly, it looked as if that might happen.

In the 2020s, a mostly White portion of the population created a political movement called the Patriot Party, in direct competition with the two traditional corporate parties.

Whites, already economically stressed, felt their privileged position was being challenged. Gender equity movements were at their peak; many males realized that their preferential status was also at risk. Quite a few of these unhappy people, born in analog times, were mistrustful and resentful of changes to their traditional ways of life. Others didn't want the stern certainties of supernatural religion diluted by the challenging questions of science. Conspiracy delusion remained rampant; in the midst of fires and floods and droughts, many still believed that the Warming was a hoax.

When I was your age, the Fourth of July was a very big holiday for Americans, as important as 350 Day is now. But in the mid-2020s even the Fourth became politicized, Red versus Blue. Many towns and cities staged competing Fourth of July rallies.

For those growing up then, the holiday still carries a certain historical sadness. You will study the Fourth of July in a happier context; when we celebrated the Tricentennial in 2076, our nation was finally becoming a place of freedom and security for everyone. That process had taken all of those 300 years, and it continues.

During the early century, the red states grew even more conservative on issues such as female health, gender rights, state-sponsored religion, and personal weaponry. And then in 2026, following a failed electoral season for the Patriot Party, a dozen of the US states petitioned Congress to call a Second Constitutional Convention.

The petition failed in Congress, but the Constitution was actually rather vague about exactly what was required to call a new Constitutional Convention. Wyoming drafted a petition directed at state governments, which was promptly ratified by ten of the reds. The red states declared victory and the "Second Constitutional Convention" met in the summer of 2027.

This controversial Constitutional Convention created the "ReConstitution Amendment," proclaiming the division of the United States into separate nations called the United States and the Free Christian Union. The FCU would be devoted to "Judeo-Christian liberty," and require English literacy for voting rights. Many of these states already had passed legislation around topics like women's health, weaponry, education and religion that fit into the priorities of the proposed nation.

The FCU states would not be contiguous, so the amendment proposed something borrowed from the original European Union: freedom of movement and free trade between all the former and current US states. But the FCU would have a federal government separate from the US, sharing only the military forces.

It was immediately clear that two-nation plan would have

serious economic consequences. By eliminating tax-revenue sharing with the blue states, the Free Union would be an impoverished nation requiring massive foreign aid from other developed countries, which was extremely unlikely.

Only Russia immediately moved to recognize the new entity. Russia shared many values with the Free Christian Union, but was unlikely to be a generous benefactor. The tattered nation was still struggling with declining population and dwindling oil revenues, combined with the high costs of mostly unsuccessful attempts at territorial expansion.

The "Amendment" was never ratified. And so the internet, not for the first time, filled with calls for rebellion and civil war. But by then the population of rebellious White people was aging out, and they weren't being replaced in similar numbers by White Gen Z.

Perhaps more importantly, by the early-Thirties, the outmigration from the biggest cities had gained momentum. A combination of climate refugees and young city people (like your nonno) moved to the alienated states, bringing attitudes that more accurately reflected modernity.

That shift in the voting population made the *official* Second Constitutional Convention possible. Convened in Philadelphia in the late 2030s, there were four Amendments: a guarantee of all-gender rights, fully public election funding, shelter and healthcare as rights, and a legal framework for digital voting to replace the electoral college.

The Patriot Party's opposition to these proposals launched the last great street demonstrations of the century as well as the Boycott Congress movement. About ten states controlled by Republicans or Patriots temporarily removed their representatives from Washington. It was only another four years until the required 38 states ratified the four new Amendments. (In the last century, it took four decades to gather enough votes for an amendment guaranteeing equal rights for women, and then the courts decided that was too late.)

The establishment of fully public election funding was perhaps the single greatest defeat for the ultrarich and the corporate powers in the US. To your generation it will seem obvious: ideas, not money, should be the fuel of elections.

AUGUST 2084

Wednesday, August 2

Every morning—before I'm out of bed, before I speak to Domo—I check my seven- and thirty-day views. Sometimes toward the end of the day, I keep the dashboard floating in my eyeline. I'm as obsessed with my stats as some young athlete preparing for their first competition.

My physical numbers are fine; dexterity and balance and gait indicators all in the happy zone.

The problem area seems to be language. Pauses, word searches, topic variances. All are creeping into the yellow.

I don't need my monitors to tell me all is not well. Of course, I've already done some research. Worst case would be Idiopathic Neural Exhaustion, a serious dementia of unknown origin.

It's seen almost exclusively in those of us age 65 to 80.

INE is probably the delayed side effect of some decades-old toxic or biologic exposure, although any evidence of the origin has long since vanished. During the War, many in my generation endured all kinds of environmental stresses—sanitation chemicals, questionable rations, toxic materials in flood waters, microscopic debris particles hurled in extreme wind events. INE is slightly more common in those of us who did cleaning and salvage, as I did those first two years in New York.

However, a viral cause is more likely. Certain viruses have long-term neural effects—polio and chickenpox, for example, in the previous century, could cause neurologic effects many years after the first infection. Those older viruses were mostly extinct when my generation was growing up. But one theory is that INE is by caused childhood exposure to the COVID-19 virus, which ran rampant in the United States.

I did test positive for COVID when I was a child; as I recall, my mother brought it home from her school, where she was required to work during the pandemic. She didn't get very sick (although they closed her school for two weeks) and like most children at the time, I showed few symptoms.

So is COVID finally catching up with me? My biggest fear is that INE might attack the so-called Broca's region of my brain, which controls language abilities and is particularly sensitive to INE. Neural implants aren't helpful and neuron regeneration doesn't usually recreate the necessary neural connections.

The exhaustion will accelerate toward the end, and ultimately damage the neurons so severely that it's no longer impossible to extract the connectome intact. Some patients, especially devout Chardinists, choose to Release and uphold before INE proceeds to its late stages.

I feel as if I am racing against something invisible, and the mind is declaring: I've said enough now.

But not yet.

FAMILY HISTORY:
NEW YORK CITY, 2020

I have one very clear memory of my own grandfather, when I was 10 or 11.

For some reason, I always called him Pops. He suffered from Alzheimer's, a progressive dementia, then a terrible scourge of older people, now quite preventable. He probably started showing symptoms when I was younger, but I didn't know anything was wrong. When I was nine, he abruptly moved from his small house out in Queens to a big brick eldercare facility, near the waterfront, in what is now the Brooklyn tidal zone.

We visited Pops on weekends, and my grandmother was always there with him. I clearly remember being surprised and puzzled when I learned that she didn't actually live there, that she was still in the old white clapboard house out in Queens where my father had grown up.

It all seemed very strange to me, as if Pops was a visitor in some hotel, but he was still funny, and happy to see me. He did get confused—I could tell him the same thing three times in an afternoon, and each time it was as if he was first hearing it. But when you're nine years old, most adults seem strange, in one way or another.

Then COVID happened. In New York the disease was particularly deadly for older people in care homes, like my grandfather. For a year, no one was allowed to visit him—not even my grandmother. After the first month or so we could see him on video; my father sent over some sort of simple video device for his room. We could just call and Pops didn't need to fuss with the complicated pads or mobiles that everyone used then.

I remember saying hello to Pops on the calls, but not much else. He survived nursing home COVID, but probably never fully understood what happened; just that his family stopped visiting. Finally, after what seemed like many months, my parents were vaccinated against COVID. And soon the nursing homes started to let people in.

Initially my parents went out to see grandfather several times by themselves. The morning of my first visit, my mother took me aside before we left the apartment. She said that Pops was sick, and that he might not remember my name. I'm sure she also said something to the effect that he loved me nonetheless. But I was still puzzling over how it could be that my own Pops wouldn't know my name. We put on our masks, walked over to the subway and took the R train out to the end of the line.

My father went into Pops' room by himself and mother and I waited in the hall. Then Dad opened the door and we both stepped inside. Pops was slouched on his sofa, looking smaller and more shriveled than I remembered him. But suddenly he saw me, straightened up and with a huge bright smile threw his arms out.

"Charlie!" he said. "Where have you been?"

Charlie was my father's name. My mother looked at me with an odd expression, nodding her head quickly, almost imperceptibly. So I stepped forward and Pops embraced me so tightly I couldn't breath. "Charlie buddy," he said softly into my ear. "I've missed you so much."

And of course, I now understand what happened. I'm glad that I didn't panic or protest, and Pops had that moment of comfort.

But at the same time, that's what I remember most about Pops. He thought I was my father, and at the time, it scared me. And that's not the kind of memory I want to leave you.

THE LAST PANDEMIC

The COVID pandemic was a key turning point in the early century, although few understood that at the time. It pushed us into the virtual world and accelerated automation far faster than either society or the technology was ready for. The pandemic threw into stark relief the inequities of our planet. For my generation, it was a powerful lesson that nature has deadly powers beyond our control and that unless we acted, far worse was yet to come.

And the final impact was that, long before individual patients were given Doubles, our species had one.

The Global Double started in the late 2020s with the Novel Disease Response network, an effort led by the EU. It's why COVID was the last pandemic on the planet. NDR was an AI that constantly monitored health information worldwide, ranging from electronic medical records and hospital visits to national health surveillance. The AI looked for any deviations from the normal local disease patterns.

NDR's first big success was identifying an antibiotic-resistant strain of pneumonic plague that emerged in Nigeria.

Even though highly contagious—the same germ was responsible for the Black Death—the outbreak was contained in less than a month. (Since then, of course, engineered alternatives to antibiotics have been developed, so you'll only see "antibiotics" in your studies.)

That left the animal-to-human viruses as potential pandemics. But we'd made progress there. During the '20s, all of the wild mammal viruses had been identified and genetically typed. Animal-to-human cases could be caught quickly and quarantined, followed by vaccine production, which could be done in under a week. That's thanks to technology pioneered during COVID, a very productive time for biotechnology. By the 2050s, zoonotic outbreaks dropped to zero, as live animal markets closed, meat consumption declined and rewilding once again separated humans from wild fauna.

If there is another global pandemic, it may well come from a different planet. But that's another essay.

FAMILY HISTORY:
TEXAS 2032 - 2034

In the early days of the War, many of my friends reenlisted in UniServ, sometimes serving six or even eight years. People in their thirties and forties enlisted also; it was hard work, but a steady job with good benefits at a time when those were scarce. For Gen Z, it was usually more interesting than what the early century called "higher education." We were learning skills that many of us would pursue for the rest of our lives.

So I reenlisted in 2032. I ended up living for two years in a work camp in what, after New York City, seemed to me the middle of nowhere: empty desert a few hundred kilometers west of El Paso, Texas. But it changed my life.

By the early 2030s, the giant carbon capture and sequestration projects—CCS for short—had started construction. The technology had existed for a decade to pull excess carbon from the air and turn it into plastics, or building materials, or even fuel for ships and aircraft. (I still have an ancient CO_2 plastic rain poncho from when I was younger—years ago I wore it for Halloween, paired with some vintage kelp-leather boots.)

But before the Strike, the corporate powers told us that carbon capture was "too expensive," particularly following the COVID recession.

After the Strike, the equation changed. Carbon capture was too expensive compared to what? Extinction?

In Texas we were building the Arrhenius Carbon Capture and Sequestration plant, named after the Swedish scientist who nearly 200 years ago first described global warming. The plant would be enormous: thirty hectares of factory floor, attached to a four hundred-hectare solar field. It was one of three-hundred carbon sequestration plants being built around the world, usually in remote areas of the middle latitudes, where giant gigawatt solar farms could provide energy for the power-hungry capture process.

The construction crew was the typical mix of National Guard, military, and UniServ, but with an unusual number of union workers. The skilled trades needed for the capture plants were the same as in the fossil fuel industry, one of the last remnants of union power in the 2030s.

So the project, even though a national emergency, still abided by some antique work rules. Which frustrated me at first—I wanted to learn how to *do* something. (In the end I did find my trade in UniServ, but not on the job.) I spent most of my time in the food hall as an "assistant bull cook," which meant I could take the eggs out of the refrigerator but not crack them. (It was some help that, in the tradition of union oil camps everywhere, the food was plentiful and delicious, and thus it was a busy kitchen.)

When I wasn't in the kitchen, I directed traffic at the worksite, gobbling salt tablets under the desert sun and waving flags at last-mile drivers operating huge trucks. The War mobilization was like, well, wartime. Supplies and equipment literally piled up in the storage facility, but with the 24/7 work schedule, there was also constant turnover.

Cargo aircraft flew into the temporary airstrip several times a day. And big automated cargo trucks cruised in from El Paso in platoons of a dozen or so, two meters between each, at a steady 120 kilometers an hour. When the trucks arrived at our work camp they would park themselves in an orderly row outside the gates. I'd dispatch last-mile drivers for the tricky task of maneuvering the trucks within the camp itself for unloading. Then the last-milers would steer the empty trucks back to the highway, point them in the right direction and send them on their way.

I should explain why we used human last-milers, either in the truck cab or via telepresence. The 2030s were a transitional period between freehand driving and automation. By then virtually all vehicles on the road, from buses to two-wheelers, were networked together. On long stretches of highway, cargo trucks could drive autonomously, in dedicated platoon lanes. But maneuvering in crowded areas where humans were also driving was much more dangerous, hence the need for last-milers. Human drivers are sometimes irrational; it requires another irrational human to keep up.

A few European countries had already made freehand driving illegal in their city centers, but the US was a bit behind. Nowadays, of course, freehand driving is illegal on public roads in much of the developed world, except for recreational tracks and some of the analog zones.

The whole dispatch and delivery process, from warehouse

to work camp, was mostly automated. But there was the occasional human error. One hot Wednesday in July, midway through my deployment, I noticed that five brand-new pickup trucks had been sitting untouched on a storage lot for at least a week.

During a break, I went over to investigate and discovered that the trucks were in fact intended for a Ford dealership in El Paso. In the frenetic pace of supplying the War, some overloaded dispatcher assumed that every new truck in west Texas was destined for the Arrhenius CCS plant.

When my shift ended, I went into the dispatch building to find someone to tell about the wayward pickup trucks. As it turned out, the clerk on duty that afternoon was a young Latina from Ohio named Marianna.

She was in her early twenties, perhaps 160 centimeters tall (or "five foot two," as the songs said back then), slim, with straight brown hair just down to her shoulders and large bright eyes. She listened to my story about the abandoned pickup trucks, and then studied me for a moment with an amused smile.

"Well, before we report it, shouldn't we go for a drive?"

I was flustered. "I grew up in New York," I told her. "I don't know how to drive."

"That's OK, New York," she said. "I'll show you how."

Two years later we were married. We were in our early twenties then. These days that's awfully young for a lifetime contract; I know most people start with shorter commitments. But that was how it was, in the intensity of the War; we were thrown together, we were working for a cause, the future was uncertain. And I suppose we needed someone to hold onto.

We were together for thirty-five years; Marianna died ten years before you were born. It was the worst time of my life. For several years I felt as if I was walking through life in a daze. It seems better now, but I would do anything to make it possible for us to be together again.

And every single day I wish she was here to see you.

ANONYMITY

Years ago, after a lesson about the early internet, your father had a terrifying nightmare about walking through a city filled with people with no faces. I remember thinking that Dylan's screams had awakened the entire neighborhood. I am sure he and Sofia will keep a close eye on you when Tutor reaches the topic of anonymity.

We once thought it normal to wander through the virtual world without knowing who was around us. This anonymity was a root cause of many internet disorders. Under the shelter of anonymity, the network was used to accentuate differences, rather than our commonality. The corporate powers invisibly threaded their messages through every conversation. Rather than encouraging truth, anonymity fueled falsity, division, deception and propaganda.

The virtual world has not been that way for many years, because, as we physically restored the planet, we also rebuilt the virtual world. The old model of the commercial internet no longer worked for what would become our planetary nervous system, the web of sensors and satellites and AI that helps manage our world. The internet also needed to become more a public commons, and less an unruly and anonymous marketplace.

The same technical team that engineered the bandwidth slowdown during the Strike launched the TruID project: secure, unforgeable legal IDs on the internet, the virtual equivalent of early century passports or drivers' licenses. ("TruID" was similar to the word "druid," an ancient Celtic cult. The similarity launched an outbreak of conspiracy theories which, ironically, is what TruID was meant to prevent.)

The TruID standard was compatible with most existing digital id systems, such as India's Aachen, the American REAL, and the EU's eID. It was not compatible with China's National ID and, until the Soft Revolution, only senior Party members and the Chinese ultrarich were allowed to have TruID. Developing nations in Asia, Latin America, and Africa adopted TruID directly as their first digital IDs. For emerging economies, the so-called Estonian Model—a fully digital civil society—was an obvious element of national success.

By the end of the 2030s, most everyone on the planet had a secure digital identity in the virtual world. Today we use the ancestral form of personal identification: our faces, scanned in multiple wavelengths so that our identity is not just the face, but also iris, underlying muscle, tissue, capillaries. For further certainty, you can add a geneprint. These days only a few old people still have ID implants; faceprint and DNA readers are everywhere, so why get chipped?

In our virtual worlds, it is nearly impossible to imitate another or steal another's information. All information—videos, VR, images, audio—is permanently tagged with its source.

Of course, at any time you can simply shut off TruID and become *truly* anonymous in the virtual world—unlike the early century, when people who thought they were traveling as "anonymous" were actually still streaming clouds of bits behind them, generally to the benefit of the corporate powers or the autocrats.

Initially, I mistrusted the TruID movement; many progressives of my generation were still afraid of government control. But it turned out, once personal privacy is guaranteed and the threat of repressive government eases, TruIDs are actually quite natural. There are still a few reasons to temporarily shut off TruID and become anonymous, but not as many as one might think. Why would anyone listen to an opinion, or believe a fact, proffered by an anonymous entity?

With TruID as a basis, security and safety in the virtual world improved greatly during the 2030s. Your parents' Domo, for example, will be one of the first AIs you have a relationship with. And you won't think anything about the way Domo manages your house. You trust Domo.

But it wasn't always that way with domestic software. My parents wouldn't even allow video sensors in the house. When I was a kid, random people could break into these cameras and watch everything you did—and there was no way to tell if that was happening, until the anonymous intruder suddenly said something! Think how terrifying that would be. (But no nightmares, please.)

In fact, in the early century, criminals broke into networks everywhere, shops and banks and schools and hospitals and laboratories and military installations; even automobiles, once they were connected.

Now, of course, millions of watchbots constantly roam the networks, knocking on virtual doors, making sure everything is secure. The name comes from human "watchmen" who once went door to door in villages, or rotated through buildings, rattling doorknobs to make sure all was locked up. Now it seems rather obvious that watchers are a good idea in the virtual world also, but it took us decades to get to that conclusion.

A side benefit of TruID is that cash has almost vanished from much of the planet: Face plus the touch of a fingertip gradually became the way we exchange money.

The governments of the world were happy to be rid of cash, which for the most part was used by criminals and tax-evaders. Well into the 2020s, the US Treasury had a lucrative business selling $100 paper currency to the rest of the world. These pieces of paper cost little to make, sold for full face value, and almost all disappeared into the underground economy, never returning to the formal banking system.

I have a small collection of mint-condition early-century currency I'll show you some day. The printing is absolutely remarkable, done not for decorative purposes but to prevent "forgery."

Most governments chose not to take cash away from their citizens. Too often cash became a matter of principle, a perceived freedom that was strongly defended—but rarely actually used. Rather than ban cash entirely, governments simply made the alternatives simpler and more attractive.

The US, for example, retired the penny in 2026 and the

nickel in 2031. Merchants were still free to price a cup of coffee at, say, $3.95, but if you wanted to pay cash it was rounded up to $4.00. When some countries began to withdraw cash entirely in the late 2040s, hardly anyone but coin collectors noticed. Today in most of the world cash is used only by the analog cults.

The rise of digital currency was another blow to the ultrarich. Governments could easily track wealth as it moved around the world. All the tax havens and secret banks and shell corporations that had, for a century, held trillions of dollars away from the world, were gradually exposed to daylight.

At first, TruID did raise concerns about a controversial topic in the early century: privacy. In times when people were not free (that is, most of recorded history), when our development as individuals was constrained by religious or social or familial expectations, a lack of privacy could be stifling or even dangerous. Hence for millennia young people left their small towns for the anonymity of the big city, where they would be free to grow their true selves.

The central concept now defined in law is that individuals have an inalienable right to choose whether or not to reveal personal information. And it turns out that what one considers "private" is not an absolute. Some want to keep even their musical preferences private; other people have lives that are in constant public view as entertainment. There are, of course, carefully regulated exceptions to the rule for investigations of criminal conduct, but these are rare.

In a way, privacy has returned to what we had early in our evolution. Whether we lived in nomadic tribes or agricultural villages, we knew the identities and many details of every person in our lives, and they knew ours. There was strength in that familiarity. We know now that in both the virtual and analog realms too much privacy can be as damaging as too little.

Tuesday, August 22

Sofia dropped in this morning while I was working on an essay. "News about Luca!" she said.

It's official: Next month, you'll be introduced to your Tutor. That's a big moment in a child's life, a coming-of-age triggered by a neural scan and the agreement of your teachers, almost always between five and six years of age. When I was a child, youth education had what seemed an endless set of stages, abbreviated as "K-12." That was really an artifact of mass education; the progress of education is never so categorical. Educators say that there should be as little distinction as possible between education, work, and life.

Tutor will be your first deep relationship with an AI, other than chattering with Domo at home. Most kids accept Tutors as if they're the most natural things in the world. You'll keep the same Tutor for life; or rather, that's the theory, since the Tutor program itself is only thirty-five years old.

Your Tutor's face will look a bit like your father's Tutor William, but not exactly. Each student's avatar is optimized. That means a similar-gendered avatar, based on one of a few dozen standard models, modified with visual aspects of your parents and yourself. That's mixed with an equal amount of otherness, racial elements not present in your family. Both your father and I always found Tutor William's face and voice very calming and reassuring, and I am certain you will have similar feelings for your Tutor.

I still feel great fondness and gratitude for my first and only Tutor, although she was a very primitive version from years ago.

I was in my early forties, your father was two years old, and I wanted to be able to teach him a bit of reading myself, before he met his Tutor. Perhaps I was still trying to prove something to my parents, both of whom were devoted readers.

The Tutor that taught me to love reading and writing was named Alice, and she was very limited compared to what you'll have—no avatar, just a friendly synthesized voice. And she wasn't formally called Tutor then. She was simply software, high-level AI designed for adults who had never mastered reading and writing in early schooling. Which was an unfortunately high percentage of my generation, since most of us had studied in the collapsing public education system, surrounded by video distractions.

Alice was humorous, patient, and extremely observant. She made up assignments based on my daily life, helped me through spelling and punctuation. After the first few weeks I actually looked forward to my daily meeting with her. And of course, I could always call on Alice whenever I was reading or writing on my own, and there she was, looking over my shoulder.

Alice constantly tracked my eye movements and recorded the ways I regularly went astray in my reading and writing. After she had collected two months of data, she created a customized font set to install on all my devices, called AldusModified, which, thirty-five years later, I still use every day, on everything I read. Sometimes I wonder what the original Aldus, that old typesetter, would have thought about that.

After six months or so, my attitude toward reading and writing began to change. In fact, I found I had a bit of a knack for it. (Except for spelling. I can never spell words quite right, especially if they have repetitive letters. Italian spelling is the worst. The letters just jump around on the page—so while you'll never see me with an active autoparser, autospell is my best friend.)

After a year, Tutor Alice was retired from inventory and replaced with a new full-avatar version. But I didn't upgrade because I was becoming confident on my own.

As is probably painfully obvious to you by now, I began to enjoy the experience of writing. Sometimes I think that I could have become a person of letters, rather than repairing robots. So why didn't I start writing after Tutor Alice? I was still young; we had Living Income by then, and I could have applied my unused ed creds for workshops in freehand writing.

But I'd spent my early years of education as the dummy who couldn't write a simple sentence without getting words or letters out of order. Autoparser and Tutor arrived too late for kids my age. Ideas about yourself get stuck in the brain. So writing as a career just didn't seem likely.

Tutor Alice also told me that since I learned to write so late in life, I will never have the optimized neuronal connections that are created in childhood. Writing and reading would always be harder mental work for me. And indeed, I can't say that the process is pleasant, but at the end of the day I am satisfied in a way that I've never felt before.

You will suffer no such setbacks. And for you, of course, Tutor is only part of education. Analog education is the other half of school life: the pods in which you study the Three C's—communication, collaboration, and creativity, the fundamentals required to be productive in a fully automated society. At school you'll almost always work in social groups, with a human teacher rather than Tutor. Why share physical space in order to be solitary?

And you'll have conversations with both teacher and Tutor. In this way, Tutor's suggestions about lines of study and occupations are shared with your human teachers, and you'll get some early practice at discussions that include humans and AIs.

EDUCATION

Your education will be so different from mine that it might as well be on another planet. My parents were idealistic teachers, so I went to public schools. In early century America, the quality of your education was based either on where you lived or how much money you had. That's why, for my childhood and teens, we lived in an overpriced two-bedroom apartment in Park Slope, which my parents could barely afford on what teachers were then paid. (I still remember the size: 800 square "feet." Back then the US was one of the few nations on earth that still clung to a measurement system based on human body parts.)

Education in early century America was a poorly-funded system that was falling apart, creating graduates who often lacked skills like scientific reasoning and critical thought. The result was a growing population that was only marginally employable and easily controlled by political and consumerist propaganda.

The ultrarich found the latter weakness quite useful in

maintaining a gullible electorate that would cheer on corporate priorities even when they went against the voters' own economic interests. On the other hand, the lack of usable skills in many American graduates was a productivity problem for the corporates, although in the 2020s it also became a convenient excuse to eliminate human workers with automation.

I was ten when the big education meltdown happened. It was the year of COVID, and New York City was the first epicenter in the United States. When school resumed in the fall of 2020, we went to class two days a week; the other days we studied at home with virtual learning.

Back then, online learning was still primitive and not very effective, especially for less-motivated students, a category that definitely included me. Both of my parents were also teaching online, so I had to schedule my homework around their teaching schedules. We didn't have enough internet bandwidth for us all to work at the same time.

You'll wonder why we didn't just put in a repair request. But like so many things in the early century, the quality of your internet connection was based on the money you paid. Some of my classmates didn't even have good enough internet access at home to keep up their studies.

Your grandmother Marianna took her classes on a telephone device with a screen no bigger than a folded handkerchief. It was an early lesson for society that connection to the virtual world is a basic human need that should not be at the mercy of the corporate powers.

Ironically, the "blended learning" that arose as a response to the pandemic is very similar to the mix of analog and virtual we use today. You'll be with Tutor about half the week and the other half you'll work in your pod. (Pod, by the way is a term that also dates back to the COVID pandemic.)

In the COVID time, the blend of real and online didn't work very well. Educational software was primitive and teachers weren't trained to balance analog and virtual. They did their best, but that school year was a long, drawn-out educational fiasco and set many of us students back a grade or so (the last thing I needed). And, of course, many parents and school systems decided that "online education" was a bad idea.

That was wrong, but it took another thirty years to perfect the AI system we call Tutor. Now it's a fundamental part of education. Tutor observes the student's emotional responses, eye movement, pupil contraction—a whole series of clues. It also notes what subjects particularly intrigue a child. And so Tutor patterns its lessons on each student's learning modes, innate abilities, and interests.

It is as if one of the finest teachers in the world was permanently assigned to each child, customizing every hour of learning to precisely fit the student's nature and inclinations.

And since Tutors are for life, your father still has his Tutor William. Tutors stay in touch with their pupils throughout their careers. Pupils who thrive in the workplace provide useful data for schooling the next generation. If a student has occupational difficulties later in life, Tutor can suggest alternatives. The lifetime education stipend per person is twenty years, and it's considered a bit wasteful not to use all of one's ed creds. It's possible to obtain an extension for up to five years, although lifetime student status is discouraged, and accompanied by a decrease in Living Income.

In a sense, Tutor is a return to the past. Centuries ago, the very wealthy employed full-time live-in tutors, instructing each child individually in Latin or French and literature and mathematics. Then, a few hundred years ago, came mass public education, which was a crucial step in evolution and led us to where we are today. But it was not for everyone. Some children thrived in mass education but there was little flexibility and few resources to help those of us who did not.

Now we, as a species, are wealthy enough to give each child an individual tutor, and that has made all the difference.

RELIGION

If you chose to follow no religion, you'd be following in my footsteps. My parents were agnostic intellectuals; growing up I was curious about my friends' religions, but nothing really stuck. At some point, in your pod, you'll visit all the spiritual spaces in New Williamsburg; three Christian churches, a Gaianist Circle, Buddhist and Hindu temples, a synagogue and mosque. You've already been to the Chardinist Chapel where your father meditates.

That sounds like a lot of churches for a town of fifty thousand, but some faiths share the Worship House. It's a space very similar to a retail pop-up: four active video walls, lightweight furniture, flexible lighting, lots of storage space for religious paraphernalia. I've been to a few events at New Williamsburg Worship House and it's astonishing how the space morphs to fit the faith.

It's been a turbulent century for religion. The 21st century began, of course, with the rise of fundamentalism across all the major supernatural religions—Christianity, Islam, Judaism, Buddhism and Hinduism. While the various fundamentalist denominations couldn't even agree on simple matters such as which animals to eat or how to kill them, they *did* enthusiastically concur on the benefits of female subjugation. That common theme connected extreme Christian with extreme Jew, extreme Hindu with extreme Muslim.

As you'll learn, misogynist fundamentalism was a natural but destructive defense mechanism among human males. On much of the planet our species had evolved to the point where skills, knowledge and social collaboration were far more important than physical mass and strength. And so males were gradually losing their dominance.

Privileged men, of course, still used laws and systemic discrimination to keep women from power. Less educated men had fundamentalist religion: a no-questions-allowed, divinely-proclaimed certainty of female inferiority. The dimmest and least capable male in the most remote village simply needed to adopt a doctrine, and he instantly become superior to half the population.

Slowly but inexorably, often against great odds, female education and rights began to spread across the world, particularly after the developing world was opened up by the Climate Justice Initiative, and the multi-national UniServ teams very often led by strong young women.

It became difficult to pretend that gender equality was anything other than the new reality, and so the fundamentalists found an increasing number of females slipping out of their control. As older fundamentalist males died off, younger recruits found the other strictures of the sects— rigid religiosity or bans on activities like dancing or alcohol—far too confining. Without the payoff of sanctioned female subjugation, fundamentalism lost much of its appeal.

Worldwide, legacy church attendance continued to decline, particularly in the chaos of the Thirties and early Forties. We had a single chapel at the carbon plant sequestration site, with services for various denominations through the week, but even in the early Thirties attendance was sparse. As the loudest voices on the national scene, the Christian extremists had done much to tarnish that brand. In general, even the moderate mainstream supernaturals found their doctrines increasingly difficult to sell to the young, who had grown up in an environment so shaped by science.

The newer suburban megachurches still attracted large congregations but did not have the sustaining wealth of the legacy religions. So the megas began to expand into businesses like life insurance, investment management, clothing, and real estate development. In the late 2020s, investment bankers urged several commercially successful Christian megas to go public as "lifestyle brands."

It was inevitable that in the late 2030s, as the cost of decarbonization and refugee resettlement continued to increase, governments began to look at the financial status of churches. The most commercial or politically active denominations lost their nonprofit status and became taxable entities. Much of the institutional edifice of organized religions fell away under the pressures of balance sheets, tax returns, auditors and the occasional fraud investigation.

The downsizing of organized religion was similar to the mid-century reduction of the great corporate powers into smaller, more socially responsive units. For the legacy religions, it was a long-overdue embrace of a humbler and more pious role. Less acceptable bits of dogma about gender roles or creation myths were quietly edited, replaced by renewed emphasis on community, cooperation, and stewardship of the earth.

Then the rise of Nous created an entirely new kind of spiritual experience. There was no plausible scientific explanation for how the Internet had grown to subtly connect billions of human consciousnesses. (Nor is there today. The most promising theory is some undiscovered elementary particle that conveys thought rather than energy, but the search for the missing "thought particle" has produced no results.)

A few of the oldest supernatural religions denounced the idea of Nous as a "false god." But Nous was no more a god than was the opposable thumb: it was a step in human evolution, a shift in consciousness.

The subtle healing properties of Nous also hinted that evolution, while often ruthless, might be driving our species toward a higher moral ground and a kinder social structure. That further contradicted the traditional religionists who depicted human nature as an inherently violent force that must be controlled by divinely-issued commandments.

Perhaps evolution *was* the commandment.

SEPTEMBER 2084

Friday, September 15

This morning I got in a bit of trouble with Dr. Leah. I was sitting in the diagnostic booth at the wellness center, having my vitals scanned in high resolution, as I do every month or so.

I brought up INE, which is sometimes now called post-COVID dementia.

On the active wall, the doctor shook her head and smiled. "Too much research. Honestly, you are only slightly symptomatic. We don't even have a firm diagnosis yet," she said. "It's far too early to talk about anything like that."

Dr. Leah looked down and continued to study my numbers. The vitals scanner cheerfully prompted me to sit very still for ten seconds. I took a deep breath and closed my eyes until the completion tone. When I opened my eyes Dr. Leah was gazing at me with a bit of amusement.

"Aldus," she said, "do you know that your dashboard reference profile for fluency has been reset to 50 years of age?"

"Sure," I told her. "That's what I keep it at."

"I hate to be the one to tell you, but you're a little older than that. As in, 50% older."

I explained that I really only became comfortable with writing when I was assigned Tutor Alice in my early forties. Since I had a late start on language, I figured I should adjust my chronology.

"Well," she said, still smiling, "that's not really how it works."

I did have one other question. "Do you happen to know at what stage dementia makes upholding impossible?"

Now Dr. Leah was staring at me a bit quizzically. "What makes you ask that?"

"I don't know," I shrugged. "I guess I'm a mechanic at heart. I just like to know how things work."

"Marianna was upheld, correct?"

"Yes."

She nodded. "First of all, I don't know the answer. There is a point where it becomes impossible but a neurologist would know better. But I have to say, I don't know why you're even thinking about this. All your verbals are within normal range for someone your age."

"But they are dropping, I know that. And my Double alert is still in force."

"And you are aging! Go home and stop worrying!"

I didn't like the "someone your age" part.

I need to finish these essays soon. If my verbals deteriorate more, I refuse to use an autoparser to help me along. I know, everyone augments their text, and not doing so makes me a dinosaur.

I worked much harder than most to find my voice and

I'm not going to settle for an autoparser's imitation. The last time I ran a match type on my prose, it came back as some gibberish like Early 20C Literary with colloquial modulation, plus extra gain on ironic inflection.

That may sound precise, but it doesn't sound like me. No professional person of letters uses an autoparser...no matter how you tune it, there's a sameness, a flatness to the voice. Sure, the individual sentences might be clearer and more focused than what 95% of the population can produce freehand. But the language is inevitably bland.

So I will carry on with my stubborn analog ways.

I will also keep an eye on my dashboard to make sure I know if my time is running out. My Double will notice long before I do. And if I need to request Release and upholding, I will.

Or perhaps my Double's hunch will prove unfounded, and I will live on to a ripe old three-digit age, in which case I have decades to finish this doc. But I'm going to continue as if I have, well, a deadline.

FAMILY HISTORY:
MARIANNA 2029 - 2045

Your grandmother Marianna was a remarkable woman, and one of my greatest regrets is that you will never meet her.

She graduated from high school in June of 2029, just three months after the Strike. In September she put college plans on hold and enlisted in UniServ. Delaying college was a big decision—she had been awarded a "full scholarship" from a private school, which meant she would pay very little for what was usually an extremely expensive education. Back then, scholarships were a rather scattershot attempt at reducing educational inequity.

Marianna's first two years in UniServ were in recovery and relocation, working with families that had been in the path of the historic Mississippi and Gulf Coast floods of 2026.

By the end of 2031, there were five Midwestern refugee camps of about fifteen thousand people each, assembled by the National Guard and the Army Corps of Engineers. The facilities—clinics, schools, food halls, etc.—were operated by UniServ recruits.

Once the facilities were completed, the military

construction teams moved on to clear the Greater Mississippi Flood Plain for long-term soil stabilization with flood tolerant vegetation. (There is now a beautiful Lower Mississippi National Park, on five thousand acres of naturalized floodplain.)

Marianna's squad leader quickly recognized that, besides being bilingual, she was also an intuitive social connector. She was assigned to help integrate refugees into established communities in the rural Midwest safe zones, and held posts at several small towns receiving refugees from the Iowa and Missouri camps. The camps were beginning to empty as refugees were resettled, either into existing housing in safe zones or the new walkables being built across the Midwest.

Marianna's job was challenging. The newcomers were a mix of climate refugees and voluntary outmigrants from the coastal flood zones, often people of color. Some of the middle states still dominated by Republicans or the Patriot Party were resistant to the newcomers. But even the reluctant states found the Federal redevelopment money difficult to turn down.

The United States had long fancied itself a "cultural melting pot." Marianna found it odd that our country had never systematically researched the best community practices for making it happen. How do you weave together the strands of different life experiences into a coherent identity: a diverse yet unified species?

Two years of resettling climate refugees were a great laboratory. She worked with schools, churches, and local business groups, and was in dozens of refugee households every week, coordinating job searches and school enrollments as well as organizing neighborhood social and online gatherings.

Marianna reenlisted and was transferred to the Texas CSS site, where we met. Her assignment there was harmonizing the young recruits, many of color, with the older and more tradition-bound union workers. As it happened, the day I met her at the storage depot she was doing a substitute shift for a friend who was ill. A very lucky coincidence. The rest, as they say, is history.

After UniServ, when we settled in New Williamsburg, she started at Ohio State and, as an undergraduate, wrote two papers on applied anthropology that are still cited today.

When she graduated, Marianna became interested in psychology and counseling as well as community work. She still had ed creds, of course, so she began to study and intern. By the time she had her credential, psychological care as a right was fully established. Like so many jobs, the need had always been there, but public counseling was chronically underfunded in the corporate economy.

AI therapists were by then sophisticated and widely accepted. For many patients the non-judgmental ear and basic insights of a virtual counselor can be more helpful than a human. But there is still a unique role for human counselors, particularly in emerging practice areas, such as the integration of analog and virtual lives.

Marianna was particularly interested in virtual partnerships and marriages. Perhaps it was because she'd had relatively few virtual relationships in her youth, compared to most of Gen Z. Her family, new to the United States, was close-knit and lived in an insular community near the meatpacking plant where her father worked.

For the first part of her childhood, the family's access to the internet was via a handheld telephone device with very limited capability. (The government provided these free to low-income people, but "free" provided only a certain amount of bandwidth per month, which back then was strictly measured.) When Marianna was eight, the family bought their first computer and for Marianna it was a revelation: her parents were video-chatting with relatives in Guatemala every week. To a little girl it was as if the world had suddenly shrunken, in a good way.

I've always thought that Marianna's interest in virtual marriage was ironic. She and I were that rare couple who got it right the first time. Sometimes I wonder if that's because we met and came to know each other in analog.

When I was young, I was never that adept on the socials, although I was very good at gaming. I still remember my parents' reaction when, at sixteen, I told them I was thinking of going pro. It was a very short conversation.

But I did meet my first girlfriend on a social called Twitch. She was what we called supersmart, and went to a fancy high school called Stuyvesant; I guess I've always liked women who are smarter than I am.

That was a pretty short relationship. I went to what my parents called a "less rigorous" high school, in Brooklyn. They weren't impressed that both Biggie Smalls and Jay-Z were alumni, and it probably doesn't mean much to you, either, although I thought that lineage was, as I would have said at fourteen, awesome.

Once again: Generation Zzzzzzzzzzzzz.......

Back to your grandmother. Virtual marriage became a specialty in her practice. The first wave of virtual marriages in the 2020s were not always exemplars of healthy relationships. In those early days, the crude state of intimate technology meant that entirely virtual marriages suggested, at the very least, a bit of emotional conflict around physical contact. But times—and technology—have changed since then.

The patients who intrigued Marianna the most were in low-touch virtual relationships. Clinically, that means relationships in which the couple (or threesome or ménage) meets in analog less than a total of one week per year. Those relationships, via active walls and VR avatars, are often a decade or more old and deeply committed.

Marianna was among the first therapists to insist on the use of the word "analog" for the physical world. She believed that "real" was a subjective term. For people who have chosen virtual marriages, or who spend most of their days in avatar communities, virtuality is more "real" than the real world. We all live in a blend of the real and virtual. "Analog" makes it clear we are talking about an experience that has no digital bits involved. "Real" is a judgment; "analog" is precise. Philosophers have said it for millennia: Reality is indeed an illusion.

One thing hasn't changed about love and marriage: for Marianna's patients, virtual or analog, sex was almost always an issue. But even sex is something that has probably changed more in my lifetime than in a dozen centuries earlier.

When I was a teenager, the virtual options were video sex or sexting. Popular, of course, but rather static. Intimate peripherals are now remarkably good. At first what was then called the porn industry drove the technology, but then in the early 2030s a physician designed very sophisticated intimate contact aids for remote sex surrogate therapy.

Intimates are still sometimes called "Dr. Dentons," after that long-ago medical entrepreneur; "wearing Dr. D" is an old-time euphemism. Medical grade intimates are still the nicest, form-fitting, comformable to various appendages and orifices, always very responsive.

Like many parents, Marianna and I bought a starter set of intimates for your father, when he was 15. From late-night discussions with him I know that almost all of his friends lost their virginity twice—once in the virtual world and then, sometimes several years later, in analog.

By 2045 or so, Marianna began to return to her original specialty, resettlement, this time with the analog cults. That turned out to be a fatal choice.

VIRTUAL LOVE

The couples who truly wrote the book on virtual marriage, in one case quite literally, were severely disabled people. In the late 2030s, in medical trials in several different countries, patients who would never again accomplish physical movement—in many cases without sight or hearing as well—were fitted with a range of brain and spinal implants, cochlear transducers, digital optic nerves and a half-dozen other neural connections. The patients could then build and inhabit full avatars in a virtual world, in which they could participate in a range of activities from athletics and music to travel, socializing, romance, and sex.

The ReVival Project was experimental, expensive, and irreversible. Much early funding came from the remaining tech conglomerates, who had an obvious interest in physically wiring as many humans as possible into their networks. As it developed, neural implants are not as safe, reliable, or accurate as the early century technologists had promised, and even today implants are used almost exclusively for medical conditions. Neural implants are surgery, and one can never be certain exactly how surgery will turn out.

The work with severely disabled people, however, was a great success and continues to this day—although candidates for full-implant virtual lives are less common. With stem cells and gene editing and 3D tissue printing, we can repair many injuries that would have once been permanently disabling. But certain fine details of human biology have proven far more difficult to manipulate than inanimate matter. Every year there are still thousands of accident victims for whom no amount of bioengineering and adaptive robotics can restore meaningful function.

For these people, living together as graceful avatars in shared virtual homes, working at the virtual occupations that suit their skills, is a far more attractive alternative than the treatment bays they inhabit in the physical world. Their best prescription is an entirely virtual existence.

Of course, able-bodied people sometimes ask for similar treatment. But total neural implant immersion into the virtual world cannot be reversed and also shortens the patient's physical life by decades. Medical and psychological approval is required and not easily granted.

In the late 2040s, a young woman with severe disabilities wrote a classic book on virtual romance called *Limitless Love*—a beautiful series of essays about disembodied love as an emotion that transcends physicality. It is still commonly read and quoted by the young and romantic, and was one of Marianna's favorites.

THE ANALOG CULTS

Analog cults emerged in the early 2030s, as our lives moved into the virtual world. The common element among the cults is total disconnection from the digital world.

Part of the motivation was the decline of anonymity, which made online malinformation more difficult to sustain. Some analogists also wanted to avoid UniServ, which they considered a globalist plot to subjugate the planet. Hardcore TruID refusers found that without a valid ID, there were limits to what they could do in the virtual world.

Today's analogists don't share a single clear ideology. Some grew out of religious fundamentalism, others the antiscience movement, or right-wing extremism, or survivalism. The cults were also important early outposts for the more extreme members of the Patriot Party and conspiracy delusionals, as they were filtered out of the virtual world by identity and veracity requirements.

Several modern faiths also have sabbath days in which they abstain from the virtual world, and many secular people do as well; when I was younger I spent a year or so observing digital sabbath. But once-a-week sabbaths are far less challenging to society than the analog absolutists.

Analogists must carry their health records and personal identification on paper and cannot be employed in most jobs. They receive their Living Income in a special form of cash, one of the last physical currencies in circulation. For many aspects of daily life, they use digitaries, who do the personal tasks that can only be done in the virtual world. Digitaries are for the most part tender-hearted volunteers, since the analogists usually have little extra income to spare.

All share the basic belief that the virtual world, and especially Nous, is a force of evil, either the creation of the devil, or mysterious elites, or out-of-control AI. Analogists believe that the virtual world will ultimately seduce and enslave humans. For many analogists, "digital" and "virtual" are actual profanities. In the early century the cults often focused on TruIDs, which in parts of the US were seen as the mark of Satan.

Self-sufficiency is also important for the analogists, in the expectation that modern society will soon collapse for one of various reasons—the arrival of a supernatural being, or a world dictatorship by AI, or some sort of massive social upheaval. Certain analogists still believe they are a separate and superior off-shoot of human evolution. (At least, the ones who believe in evolution.) "You will not replace us" is one analogist slogan, dating from the early century, long before the cults themselves.

Perhaps most importantly, pure analog life lets followers maintain the elaborate belief structures they have built over the decades, about government or science or race or gender or alien visitors. Analog ideology is the most persistent collection of conspiracy theories remaining in the 21st century, because it propagates physically—orally, or on paper, or via antique analog tape recordings—rather than in the virtual world. Thus there is little way to inject reason via media or the socials.

FAMILY HISTORY:
NEW WILLIAMSBURG 2035

There's a small greenspace in downtown, directly across the walkway from the Chardinist Chapel, that, many years ago, was called a bus stop. I'll show it to you sometime, because it always makes me remember the day that Marianna and I first arrived in town, fresh off an exceedingly dusty hydrogen bus, after a twenty-hour ride from El Paso.

That was fifty years ago, when New Williamsburg was still under construction, one of the first walkable villages. Several hundred walkables were initially built in exurban areas around the US, intended for climate refugees and UniServ veterans. Fully sustainable, on their own microgrids, each walkable was a mix of apartments, townhouses, and detached houses, a combination of rental and owner-occupied, plus retail, health, and childcare.

Under the pressure of resettling climate refugees, some of the early walkables like New Williamsburg grew too large, in our case now nearly fifty thousand. No one would propose that scale today, nor would it be necessary.

Like so many things in our rethought world, two sizes seem to work for human communities: small and giant. New Williamsburg is more the size of an early century construction, the "suburb." Suburbs were intended as a compromise between villages and cities, but they turned into sprawling, uncontrolled settlements that make no sense today.

Someday your parents will take you to see the historical Park of the Suburb in Virginia, a restored 2005 suburb, complete with original landscaping, furnishings, vehicles, schools, even a shopping mall. I went there when it opened in 2075 and it's very authentic; pure nostalgia for my generation. You will be amazed by the huge, vintage automobiles, and it has a couple of great AR exhibits: You can watch Saturday afternoon at the mall, or the bustling entrance of an elementary school during morning rush hour.

(Rush hour. I remember explaining that phrase to your father when he was 12 or so. He said: "Everyone woke up at the same time, got in their cars at the same time, and drove in the same direction? That's crazy." I couldn't really argue with him.)

Anyway, I digress, as I tend to do these days.

Besides our UniServ housing voucher, Marianna qualified for a retention bonus, paid to keep young locals in the middle states. She was definitely a local. Her father Juan (your middle name) had immigrated from Guatemala to Ohio in the early century to work in an animal meat-packing plant. After COVID, he was promoted to be a health coordinator. (Marianna's older brother is a biochemist at a meat bioreactor in Illinois...she used to joke that "meat" is the family business.)

So Marianna was coming home to Ohio. But I was leaving New York, the only place I had lived before UniServ.

I loved growing up in New York—the entire city was a classroom. When I was a teenager, Brooklyn was alleged to be the epicenter of all that was cool and trendy. The Parisians even praised style as "très Brooklyn." Your hometown, New Williamsburg, like many of the early walkables, took its name from a then-fashionable Brooklyn neighborhood. It was a joke at the time, although the name stuck.

Leaving the city was less painful than I'd thought. As soon as I started college, my parents had moved to southern Michigan, to live near your great-grandmother. As public-school teachers they earned too little money to buy a New York apartment or maintain a comfortable life. Although it makes no sense now, most teachers were very poorly paid in the early century.

My parents departed Brooklyn reluctantly. But they had plenty of company on their way out. On both US coasts, deurbanization had started post-COVID and then accelerated with virtualization over the next two decades. Part was involuntary outmigration, as the coastal cities cleared people out of flood plains. But much was by choice.

I'm not sure why anyone in the early century believed that cities would just keep growing as they were. Tiny apartments for millions of dollars, private schooling for toddlers that cost as much as an automobile? The inequities were, in retrospect, astonishing, yet the corporate powers and the developers insisted: taller buildings, more people, less space, higher cost. Perceived scarcity meant bigger profits and a more compliant workforce.

But the historic momentum of urbanization began to slow and then gently reversed. Over the first half of the 21st century, the American Midwest and South gradually repopulated, as well as the small villages of Europe. More recently, in Africa, Asia, and Latin America, there has been movement from the awful megacities back to traditional small-scale communities. Thanks to the Climate Justice work during and after the War, these villages now have electricity, clean water, treated sewage, telemedicine bays, and full local language Tutor connectivity.

In the U.S., the first to deurbanize en masse was Gen Z and our younger siblings. Many of us left New York, Boston, Los Angeles, Chicago, to live in the new walkables in Kansas or Ohio or the south. If we worked in urban pursuits like design or advertising, we could easily do so from home or in local telepresence centers.

For physical work, you could tend robots in a distribution warehouse, or monitor the irrigation in a vertical farm, or manage the nutrient broth in some bioreactor. Or repair robots, as your nonno Aldus does. As you will learn, many of those jobs were automated in the 2030s and 2040s, but when Living Income was enacted, the walkables were also ideal settings to pursue the arts and skilled crafts.

In a sense, the city came with us. By the time Marianna and I were settled in New Williamsburg, the most chic artisanal food pop-up could be replicated anywhere in the country, in a matter of days, with active video walls, 3D printing, and similar virtual retail tricks.

Even the famous New York Broadway theaters (choosing to diversify their business model post-COVID) streamed VR performances several nights a week—theater from tenth row center; dance and music, the fifteenth. The bulky VR capture rigs took up half a dozen prime seats—but filled those seats with thousands of virtual show-goers from across the country.

Often including your grandmother and me.

REVISITING NEW YORK

I enjoy my visits to New York, but I no longer feel a tug at my heart. New York was always changing, not always for the best, and this time it is different indeed.

When I was a kid in New York, half the city seemed to be perpetually under construction. Post-COVID, it slowed substantially. Then, in the 2030s, with all the federal War funding, it started again. But it wasn't like the early century, when developers built enormous condominiums for the ultrarich, or flashy insubstantial apartment buildings my progressive parents called "yuppie filing cabinets."

These early century buildings, designed for looks rather than resilience, were soon deteriorating under the onslaughts of rain bombs, derechos, hurricanes, extreme temperatures, the occasional urban tornado. In a matter of a few decades, the buildings required complete renovation, and often repurposing. For example: several of the costly condominium towers that once housed Wall Street princes and Russian oligarchs had their height cut in half and became vertical farms.

New York City also rebuilt some of the coastal zones devastated by Hurricane Belinda, creating new neighborhoods that borrowed ideas from the walkables for resilience and livability.

What made coastal zone reconstruction possible was the biggest single New York City project in history: the Hudson and East River tidal surge barriers. The Outer Harbor Gateway stretches from a barrier island in New Jersey to the tip of Long Island in New York; the Upper East River Barrier cuts across Long Island Sound.

These gigantic grey behemoths heave up out of the ocean like surfacing whales to block the worst of the tidal surges. The barriers are named Revelle and Keeling, after two early Warming researchers. The tidal dams are engineering marvels, but still require a staff of nearly five hundred simply to mitigate the environmental impacts on the Sound and the rivers; saving New York City had a very high price tag.

All around the country, in fact, the cost of saving the coastal cities was enormous, both in financial and psychological terms. I think when you grow up in a coastal city, you have always have this subliminal sense of where the ocean is—some inborn homing signal. When I used to visit California, I always felt like the ocean had been moved to the wrong side.

Now when I visit New York City, I feel like the Atlantic Ocean has also moved. You feel it, but now pushed away to arm's length. At least for my lifetime. Or is it forever?

We don't know. We'll find out in what is sometimes called the "unforeseeable future." For all our science and quantum modeling and satellite surveillance, we really don't know the long-term state of our oceans.

In the decades since the first 350 Day, of course, global temperatures have dropped. No one expected a sudden change, but it's happening, and accelerating a bit in the last decade. But the oceans will hold deep reservoirs of heat for decades more. What is left of the icecaps has stabilized but isn't growing. A few of the ancient great glacier fields, set for certain extinction, remain in diminished form, geophysical seeds that give hope for glacial regrowth—perhaps beginning in your new century. But we will likely never regain the rich, lovely coastlands that our ancestors grew up with.

New York, though, was lucky by comparison to the American Gulf Coast.

The coastline of the Gulf states would be unrecognizable to a visitor from the early century. While we haven't seen a Category 6 for a decade now, strong hurricanes are still a part of southern coastal life. Some of the stabilized storm surge corridors go so far inland that they actually meet the Mississippi flood plains—it's this beautiful band of land, sometimes forty kilometers wide from ocean's edge to the inland safe zones.

And then, in the midst of those green bands, every thirty kilometers or so, are the safe ports. All the way from Apalachicola in Florida on the east to Galveston, Texas on the west you'll see the tall tidal dams and the elevated locks that carry ocean freighters from sea level, ten meters up, to meet the Inland Waterway channels.

Well; once again I digress. The Atlantic coastline may not be quite what it was, but I still like to visit New York—it's two hours by maglev from the Columbus station. New York remains a lively and fascinating city, a center for the arts and intellectuals, although smaller than when I was growing up.

And it's so much easier to get around than in the early century. All of Manhattan ground transportation is automated; it was one of the first American cities to ban freehand driving, although the last-mile drivers union fought that in court for years. Two, ten, and twenty-person vehicles are routed on surface streets in real time; Transport gives riders the quickest, cheapest choice. If you're a regular commuter, Transport automatically learns your patterns and matches those with proximity information.

What still amazes me most are the silent subway cars, thanks to the maglev rail conversion in the 2060s. Riding between stations, all you hear is the soft hum of the magnetic fields that provide propulsion, and the rush of air against the windows. Even after twenty years, I can never quite believe my ears.

Tutor once gave your father a history lesson that showed a crowded, noisy, lurching New York subway car from back in the 2020s. Dylan covered his ears from the din and later, when I asked him about it, he said: "It was SO LOUD that everyone in the car had EARPLUGS, on strings around their neck."

I explained that those weren't earplugs, they were "earphones" for sound. And the "strings" were actually metal *wires* that were used to carry electricity—a new fact that your father immediately found far more interesting than some noisy old underground train.

FAMILY HISTORY:
NEW WILLIAMSBURG 2059

Shortly before I turned 50—I don't recall exactly when—your grandmother Marianna came back from evening meditation at the chapel and said she had something serious to talk about.

I was immediately concerned. Marianna had strong ideas, but she was also deft at presenting opinions with a relaxed tone, a bit of humor. She rarely made so abrupt a preface.

Marianna sat beside me, cross-legged on the old couch in our living room, pushed her hair back and touched my knee. "I'm sorry," she said, smiling, "you look like you just heard you were being offlined tomorrow. I didn't mean to worry you. The topic today was the infinite nature of Nous and as I was meditating, I suddenly realized that I want you to be upheld also."

Marianna was by then devoted to Chardinism. The Chardinists were among the first to adopt upholding, when the science of connectome preservation emerged in the late 2040s. Upholding was something the old Jesuit Teilhard de Chardin could never have imagined, but it was nonetheless widely embraced by the faith. There was even a special Upholding Service following the procedure; I'd been to several of these for older congregants who had become friends.

I told Marianna I hadn't really thought about it, and she straightened up and grew intense. "We compost our bodies and transform them into trees or meadows or reefs. But what respect do we show our minds?"

Your grandmother and I had talked about her decision for several years, and I never had a strong opinion one way or the other. I barely knew what a connectome was, and it seemed like something that we would not have to worry about until the distant future.

To be honest, I don't fully understand upholding, even now. I'm sure you'll someday learn about it from Tutor, unless we invent some new theory before then. The connectome is the mathematical pattern of the connections between the billions of neurons that create a mind: it's pure data. The connectome is the software essence of consciousness.

Upholding captures and stores the connectome. In the procedure, an electrical current is pulsed through the brain, generating a software model of the neurons and synapses. The voltage level damages brain tissue, so it's performed only after natural death or Release. Upholding needs to happen within the first few days after death, before neural deterioration has taken place, or the data will be corrupted. Prolonged dementia also creates serious flaws in the software.

If I have my connectome upheld, as Marianna asked, we'll both reside as patterns in a dedicated neural network storage cloud. At that point the connectome is beyond any human contact—we have no idea how to interface with this disembodied data.

Cloud maintenance workers do find some very low electrical activity among the stored connectomes: a small amount of bandwidth flowing in and out, almost like blood. We have no idea whether that's a simulacrum of "thinking," or perhaps some form of communication between the connectomes, or merely some low-level technical refresh mechanism.

In any event, researchers have been unable to extract any meaning from those signals, even after years of work in what skeptics sometimes call "séance science."

The night that Marianna brought up the topic, I remember feeling very uncomfortable. We were still young. I didn't like the entire premise of the discussion. "Let's not get ahead of ourselves," I said. "All that is so far in the future that it makes my head hurt to think about it."

"I know," she said softly. But she was relentless. "You just have to promise."

So I promised. And it is a promise I intend to carry out, one way or another.

I suppose for devout Chardinists, it's comforting to know that a loved one's connectome is integrated into the digital body of Nous. And of course I'm glad that Marianna's final wish was accomplished. My question: do we expect these connectomes to someday be activated again?

We don't know. Science still finds that true human consciousness can only exist in a mortal physical body.

Perhaps it will be different in your life and there will be some way to revive connectomes into consciousness. Or will Nous evolve further, with some unknown role for our connectomes? Either is possible. After all, who in the early century might have imagined Nous?

CHARDINISM

When it grew clear in the 2050s that Nous was real, if still mysterious, it seemed to require a new spiritual framework. There was a burst of start-up religions, but the most successful was based on the writing of Teilhard de Chardin.

The faith grew so quickly, in fact, that I was suspicious; I am not a follower of crowds. But de Chardin's thinking fit the 21st century well, as a spiritual basis for the origins and direction of evolution, and the belief appealed immediately to Marianna, since the original source was a Catholic priest.

Your grandmother was raised as a Roman Catholic. Her mother was born in the Guatemalan highlands and so there were threads of Mayan belief threaded into her Catholicism, particularly some unconventional saints. Those saints had nothing to do with Rome, and were likely stand-ins for Mayan entities that had been around since long before Christendom. I distinctly remember that when I first visited Marianna's parents in Columbus, her mother had a statue of a saint wearing a stylish fedora, smoking a cigarette and holding a bottle of rum. Thus Marianna was accustomed to improvisation in her Catholicism.

De Chardin was an early 20th century Jesuit, censured in his lifetime by the Church for his fascination with scientific evolution. But his theories turned out to be surprisingly prescient. Very devout Chardinists even consider de Chardin a prophet, although de Chardin himself would likely have found the notion embarrassing.

Some Chardinists even believe that the decarbonization of Earth during the 21st century was a "miracle" created by Nous. But I think the unprecedented global cooperation of the War on the Warming was natural. With new tools like universal networking, humans were simply organizing, as instinctively as a swarm of bees might when their hive is under attack. No miracles required.

Chardin's key inspiration was his "noosphere," which built on the fundamental law that the direction of the universe is disorder and entropy. "*Spare your heart,*" says a 20th century song by writer Paul Simon. "*Sooner or later everything put together falls apart.*" We living creatures are only momentary crystals of self-organization growing up out of natural disorder. Inevitably, our molecules return to disorder: dust, ashes, soil.

De Chardin believed that decay and disorder were *not* the fate of our thoughts and knowledge. He proposed that our mental creations linger after us, adding layers to the noosphere; a mystical accretion of wisdom that sits invisibly atop the physical world, continuing to grow with each human generation, resisting entropy as the rest of the universe falls apart.

To add to the mysticism, de Chardin believed that the noosphere is taking us toward a final moment in the future when the "Omega Point" is reached, a divine consciousness that will survive even beyond the death of the universe.

The old Jesuit never imagined that we humans would actually build a digital version of his noosphere. Although perhaps he did have a premonition. Here's his quote, etched above the door of the New Williamsburg Chapel:

"Someday, after mastering the winds, the waves, the tides and gravity, we shall harness for God the energies of love, and then, for a second time in the history of the world, man will have discovered fire."

FAMILY HISTORY:
NEW WILLIAMSBURG 2060

Given her background in blending cultures, I suppose it was inevitable that Marianna was also drawn to the absolute opposite of virtual relationships: the analog cults, the most alienated people remaining in the country. The challenge fascinated her; it was also, sadly, her last work.

Marianna began to work with the analogists in the late 2050s, starting with a small colony who still live about 20 kilometers south of New Williamsburg. ("Colony" is of course a rather negative word historically, but that's actually what the analogists choose to call their settlements.) Marianna was assigned as a counselor for the "Children of Gaia" when they first settled in our area. They were migrating from an urban area of southern California, where they were very unhappy. The analog cults fare better in more rural settings.

The Children now consist of perhaps 20 families in all, fully analog, on a small farm. Their faith is a confusing blend of fundamentalist Christianity, nature worship, and survivalism. Years after Marianna worked with them, I met a few of the adult members, and they reminded me of what I have read about hippies in the last century. Naive, a bit deluded, self-righteous, but not evil, and surprisingly happy. They support themselves by growing vegetables and, during winter, handwork at home for boutique clothing designers.

In all, they seem like people who have for some reason decided to make their lives needlessly difficult. But that's nothing new for organized religion.

Marianna helped the Children settle into their farm, arranged digitary services, and worked with the surrounding community to engage with the newcomers. She also enrolled their younger children in PreK, which was very important. The law requires that all children spend their early years in the public system, usually to age six, through the early introduction to virtuality. At the point when Tutor is assigned, parents can decline and continue to educate their children at private analog academies or at home.

The upbringing of the analogist children was the most controversial element of the cults. Early public education is required because those years are so crucial for a child's mental development; it is considered a matter of community health. It's not so different than public health measures from my youth, such as vaccination requirements. More crucially, public schooling gives analogist children some experience in the virtual world. Then, if they ultimately adopt their parents' belief system, it is with an awareness of their choices.

THE EMERGENCE OF NOUS

You'll take Nous for granted, when you are older. But there was a time, before Nous had a name, that it was a mystery, gradually emerging, first suspected by a few, then thousands, then millions around the world. Now it's only slightly less a mystery, but we know it is real.

There was no one moment when Nous did not exist, and then a next moment when it did. The first signs were subtle. Initially, in the years following the World Strike it seemed, especially for those of us in our teens and early twenties, that something ineffably subtle was changing on the Internet. New ideas emerged simultaneously around the globe, novel sights seemed somehow familiar. Most strikingly, the rancorous tone and nasty edge that had always tinged so much "social" media gradually abated. Even usually cynical journalists wrote about "the rise of virtual civility".

By then almost everyone on earth was connected; during the early days of the War, Climate Justice funding brought wireless broadband to many of the final offline portions of the globe—remote areas in Africa, southeast Asia, and Latin

America. Solar-powered earth stations, connected to low-earth-orbit satellite networks, were installed in dozens of developing nations.

Then came international TruID plus autotranslation. The new coop social nets replaced their commercial predecessors. Even the major autocracies—China, Russia, the Middle Eastern states—relaxed their restrictions on global interconnection. Nations simply couldn't participate in the world without it. The planet needed a single nervous system.

Was the new equanimity of the web simply a result of the shared sacrifice of the War? Or perhaps it was the mediating effect of TruID, which eliminated the destructive uses of anonymity?

But there was something more. Occasionally, for example, I knew what someone on a social would say before they said it. As soon as some idea came into my head, unbidden, I would begin to see it everywhere. Images of distant places I'd never seen before somehow felt familiar. Psychologists dredged up the old term "promnesia." The opposite of amnesia, promnesia is the certainty that you remember something you *haven't* seen.

Then came the first scientific evidence for Nous. In 2039, in a popular social devoted to dream interpretation, members realized that they were experiencing exactly the same dreams. A sleep researcher started to document the number of occurrences—dream duplications that were not just similar, but exact. In a dream about starlings, it wasn't a vague number of birds, or a flock, but exactly a dozen. This repeated hundreds of times in the dreams of the participants.

It happened particularly among Zs and our younger

siblings. A few years after your grandmother and I moved to New Williamsburg, for example, I remember a dream about some random set of objects—an old-fashioned schoolhouse, a garden shovel. In the morning, I mentioned it to your grandmother, and she told me that she had the same dream two nights before.

Later that day, I heard the same dream from a fellow student at school, in my mechatronics workshop. It was the first time it had happened to any of us, although of course we'd heard about it. It was unsettling, even though we knew it was not just us.

By the mid-2040s, tens of thousands of dream duplication episodes were arriving constantly from around the world. Scientists initially deemed it coincidence. Given a big enough population, such coincidences were mathematically quite likely.

Yet the phenomenon continued and turned into a sensation—*ShareDreams* was the tag—as millions of people, across the planet, in a dozen languages reported identical dream images.

Science switched to a new hypothesis: "mass delusion." Similar shared follies had swept populations before, although never the entire planet at once. But in the winddown days of the War, when all of life still seemed turned upside down, a bit of communal madness was understandable. These reports, after all, were based on recollections of dreams, the most ephemeral material, easily manipulated in the receptive mind to make one dream seem "identical" to another.

Then, however, researchers at Stanford's Sleep Medicine Center launched a study. It built on much older research: Long ago, in the 1970s, a handful of scientists had conducted "dream telepathy" experiments, to determine if people were more likely to receive telepathic images while in the dreaming stage of sleep. The results had been mixed and there were few follow-up studies; soon psychic research of all varieties fell out of favor.

The new Stanford shared-dream research studied over seventy population groups around the world that had little or no internet access (some old fundamentalist sects, the early analog cult colonies, some offline tribal communities). Hundreds of interviews made it clear that no one in these groups reported an increase in sharedreams.

The new phenomena, from promnesia to sharedreams, had grown spontaneously inside the global network. It was not the Internet, or the Web, or cloud, or any of the other then-current colloquialisms. It needed a name. In 2049, a Canadian philosopher proposed "Nous" and the word gradually spread across the planet. Pronounced with a long "o" as in *ghost*, it sounded right in every language.

Nous came from early Greek—Homer used it in the Iliad, as did Plato and Aristotle, referring to pure thought. It also had linguistic similarity to the Latinate *nos*, which implies a collective.

Nous is like a river that runs through all our minds, an invisible current of thoughts and emotions that ebbs and flows in a collective subconscious. It is not thought transfer, although researchers suspect a primordial element of Nous may be behind cases of "mental telepathy" in the earlier centuries, such as the 20th century dream experiments, or those who sense that a close relative has died, often right at the moment of death. (Although I felt no psychic tremors when Marianna died; I only recall the alerts going off in my dualview, likely moments after her truck fell into the canyon.)

Many now believe that the Strike was the first embryonic stirring of Nous: the global connections were in place, the language barriers had fallen, and when the Earth's suffering from the Warming grew too great, it was as if the organism itself suddenly awoke, shocked into consciousness by the pain.

That's rather an anthropomorphic way to characterize the behavior of a planet of stone and water. But in fact, something altogether new entered our lives at the most deeply troubled moment of this century.

OCTOBER 2084

Friday, October 6

I had a great dinner at your house yesterday, along with a stern lecture from your father.

We'd planned to go to a restaurant but then your parents' meal co-op offered a last-minute special, a lemon pasta. Your mother had contributed a half-dozen Sicilian recipes to the co-op, and this one earned a regular place in the rotation.

Your mother prefers to make pasta herself, but last night she had a deadline design project and your father was in a late meeting with the Pecos foundry manager.

Ten minutes or so after I sat down, Domo announced that dinner had arrived. I still chuckle when I hear that. Fifty years ago you didn't need an announcement to know that a drone was near your house. They sounded like a massive swarm of angry hornets; sometimes people shot them out of the sky with guns.

The meal cooperatives have been another big change, started well after the childcare co-ops. Meal prep needed more technology, and the big, highly automated ghost kitchens didn't really take off until the 2030s.

Ghost kitchens—that's another phrase from the history books. Those started in big cities in the early century, when meal delivery was becoming popular. Ghost kitchens were for restaurants without physical dining rooms—all the food was delivered or picked up.

Meal delivery accelerated during COVID, and many restaurants never reopened their dining rooms. They'd have pop-up dinners in temporary spaces (there was a lot of empty commercial space in those years), but most of their business was delivery. The meal coops built on ghost kitchen technology, and were a natural extension of the food coops popular in the anti-corporate movement.

Last night's pasta was accompanied by nice pork sausages from a boutique bioreactor managed by an old Italian family in Cleveland.

Neither of your parents generally eats animal meat, although your mother insists that there has never been a synthetic prosciutto that matches natural. (She's a bit prejudiced since the farmer across the road from her childhood home makes remarkable natural prosciutto.)

You ate your pasta quickly and asked to be excused; you went off into a corner of the big common room and started playing with a favorite new toy, a model of the Space Elevator docking station, complete with five or six various orbital runabouts.

Once you were occupied with the Space Elevator, your parents and I had another discussion about my health. My dashboard indicates some deterioration, and I still feel a kind of mental exhaustion that is new to me. But it hasn't changed in the past few weeks, so I told them I consider myself stable, although I'm actually not that confident.

"I'm just going to ask you right out," Dylan said. "Are you thinking about preemptive upholding?"

"Where did you get that idea?"

"Dr. Leah told us."

I was shocked. "That's a privacy violation!"

"Dad, Dr. Leah has known you for thirty years. And we are your healthcare surrogates, remember?"

"Of course I remember." Why does everyone keep asking me if I remember things?

I explained: I have no intention of being upheld until my condition is much worse, although neither do I want it to get so bad that my connectome is too damaged for storage.

Your parents were still clearly concerned.

"Listen," your father said, trying a lighter tone. "Don't you want to see the 22nd century? You'll only be 90 then. You take good care of yourself, you could live to be 125."

"I find it hard to imagine myself as a spry 125-year-old," I told him. "The centenarian Millennials I know mostly don't look so good."

"But you're a later generation," Sofia said. "Each generation starts with more advantages."

"I know. I bet your Doubles read something like 130, maybe more."

Sofia and Dylan glanced at each other, and I knew I was right.

Someone your age, Luca, can potentially live to 140 or so; at that point, no matter how much telomere therapy we have, we're turning into androids with replacement parts. Our containers just aren't designed to last forever. Stem cell organ regeneration no longer finds a complete set of DNA blueprints to duplicate. There's also a limited lifespan to synthesized organs like the liver and kidneys; they're a lot better than the old porcine products but never as sturdy as the originals. And once patients are in the upper decades, it gets harder to connect neural implants.

I'm not going to say this to your parents, but some gerontologists speculate that even family may cease to be a motivator for extended longevity. A person of 140 could be a great-great-great-great-grandparent. Perhaps I'm cynical, but by then, the excitement of watching the next generation may be ebbing. For extreme elders, their tangle of descendants may be so large and diffuse that they wouldn't be able to recognize most of their great-great-great-great grands if they met them on the street.

Of course, what your parents weren't mentioning was the other threat to extreme elders: the new diseases that arise in one's second century. Earlier in history, for example, certain very slow cancers were seen only when people started living long enough for the disease to emerge. So it is today. We've eliminated or can treat most of the diseases that were fatal for the elderly in the early century. But as a few remaining Boomers pass 120 or so, we're seeing new disorders, still poorly understood, most involving the brain. And some new conditions are even showing up among young-olds like me. Such as idiopathic neural exhaustion.

Dylan shook his head. "Dad," he said, "Dr. Leah says INE is entirely your theory, not hers."

"Of course, I know that. I was just speculating about worst case."

"Nonno," Sofia said, "what does your friend Mena say?"

"Oh," I said, and waved one hand. I paused for a moment and Sofia interrupted.

"So she doesn't even know."

"I don't want to worry her."

Both your parents watched me in silence for a long moment. It was a bit disconcerting. "Well," I said finally, "that was a great dinner. That was the pasta you made the first night I met you in Sicily."

Sofia nodded. "I remember that very well. It was a nice evening. The first of many."

"And many more to come," I said. "I should get home."

"Dad," Dylan said, "I want you to go talk to Priest Anne about this. Promise."

The tone in your father's voice made it clear that he did not intend to start a discussion. I promised.

Before I left, I paused for a moment to watch you with the Space Elevator model. It reminded me of how you had been fascinated with the solar system model at childcare a few months ago, when I filled in for your father. I suspect you'll be a member of Space Club in a couple more years.

I know that some progressive parents have the old prejudice that Space Club is a bad influence on children, distracting them from the necessary work on our own planet. But no matter what modern parents think, the Clubs are still an improvement over the early century, when we had youth groups organized solely around gender.

I say Space Club is a great way to practice science. And there's nothing wrong with fantasizing a bit about human planetary exploration.

SPACE IS FOR BOTS

Space Club will teach you more than you'd ever want to know about our lunar and planetary adventures in the early century. But Space Club is a little weak on the question of why there aren't a lot of humans out there anymore.

Basically, it was a matter of priorities. Back in the 2030s we needed trillions of dollars every year to save our own planet. Many of us began to ask: What exactly is the point of colonizing *other* planets?

Space enthusiasts, of course, said we needed an alternative planet, should this one become uninhabitable, which in the early century appeared to be a distinct possibility. One of the ultrarich, for example, argued that we could "terraform" Mars into a livable planet. At the time it seemed clear to most young people that our first priority should be to terraform Earth.

It didn't help the spacers' case that the first public space travel was costly suborbital trips for billionaires. It was hard to avoid the conclusion that if Mars got terraformed, it was going to be a six-star resort. And the evacuation fleet from Planet Earth was not going to have economy class.

Space exploration slowed substantially in the 2030s and 2040s, as the world's technology funding focused on extreme weather defense, recovery, and decarbonization. In the early '30s, extreme weather severely damaged two American spaceports and one of Russia's key launch sites.

By mid-century, human space travel was uncommon. The human body is a very fragile object, not at all suited for interplanetary transit. Instead, we send smart robots with virtual reality transmitters. That allows thousands of trained scientists to explore other planets, rather than a few astronauts whose physical stamina and piloting prowess were more important than their research skills.

A scientist on Earth can easily don a full VR suit and jog across a lunar crater, or fly through the sulfuric acid clouds of Venus, or even swim in Mars' newly-discovered sub-terranean salt lake. In the future, as we master high-bandwidth timeshifting, it will be even better: Someday, when a researcher in Boston reaches for a rock on the surface of Mars, their robot double will reach at the same instant.

As for those dreams of space colonies, well, our historical motivation for colonies has always been financial: harvesting new resources such as gold or spices or human beings, ventures that never ended well for the indigenous inhabitants. So, what resources might we exploit on other planets? The only apparent answer was minerals. When labs like Chrysopoeia began to synthesize rare materials, there was no longer any rational reason to go dig up other planets.

The US lunar colonies, Earthside and Darkside, had a combined population of over 70 people by the 2040s, when full-time staffing was withdrawn. The cost of maintaining that many people on the moon simply outweighed the benefits. There are, of course, always a half-dozen or so people in temporary residence for maintenance or specialized research. All of the small lunar observatories—Earthwatch, Deep Space, and SolarView—are also fully automated and visited by human crews only a few times a year.

Certainly there is still a sense of bravura at the thought of a human astride another planet. That's why there are Space Clubs worldwide, supported by millions of members. But this remains a hobby for our species, at least until we have fully repaired our current planet.

Personally, I think the Space Elevator, the model you were playing with last night, is the greatest space accomplishment of our century. The satellite belts are key parts of the planet's nervous system and intelligence, so we need cheap and dependable access. Hence, the Elevator, an early century fantasy now made possible by new materials.

A 36,000-kilometer-long cable of carbon nanotube rises up from the flatlands of Kansas, through the stratosphere and into earth's high orbital plane. It is secured in space by a massive counterweight—an enormous chunk of space rock, harvested from the asteroid belt. Every day a few dozen passenger or freight climbers ride the elevator into orbit—a five-day trip.

At the top of the elevator is a permanent space station, where riders transfer into the space vehicles that are permanently parked in the orbital plane: satellite maintenance ships, space junk scavengers, even two brightly-colored (and very expensive) public sightseeing ships.

The Space Elevator is a global collaboration—the EU, the US, Russia, China, and India. It took over a decade to build and now has a staff of nearly a thousand. A second is now operating in the plains outside Chengdu, in China, and a third will be functioning in central Turkey soon.

For the first ten years after the Elevator began operation, civilian trips into orbit were an international honor. The Orbitals went to individuals who had done exceptional work on fighting the Warming. Now, the range of contributions eligible for Orbitals includes science and technology, healthcare, education, the arts, humanitarian service, and philosophy.

There are also a few slots for the paying public—very expensive, with a two-year waiting list just to get into the lottery drawing.

When I was young, working on my robotics certification, all of us wanted to work on ocean bots. Now, orbital mechatronic is one of the best jobs in technology, with thousands of applicants for each opening. The majority of those jobs are earthbound, operating and maintaining the fleets of orbital robots. But there are always unforeseen issues that require hands-on inspection, so orbital ascents are a coveted part of the job.

The "astronauts" of the early century are now mostly mechanics like me.

FAMILY HISTORY:
SICILY 2071

I was there the day your parents first met. In, of all places, an old Roman ruin in Sicily, way back in 2071.

Dylan spent the first year of his UniServ tour on the Italian island, assigned to a reforesting project. UniServ still observed the old tradition of mixing nationalities—cultural hybridization has always been a tonic for our species. One of Dylan's classmates went to the Atlas Mountains, an analog zone near Marrakech, and another friend served in a small town outside of Montreal. While your father was on a big solar air freighter traveling the 15 hours to Europe, I'm sure that some earnest young Belgian or Spaniard set off for Ohio, assigned to the Appalachian Rewilding Initiative.

At first, Dylan was disappointed that he was headed to the Old World, because Africa was the most coveted assignment for his generation.

During the worst of the Warming, east and southern Africa suffered the largest single death toll on the planet. Drought, famine and disease killed tens of millions, well past the entire planet's toll for water and wind. And then in the 2030s, western Africa began to experience unpredictable flash droughts, putting yet more stress on water supplies.

There was no way to transport enough water into the most isolated areas to save everyone. Massive aid distribution efforts during the 2030s did save millions, and a few million more were relocated to safe zones.

Then, starting in 2040, a huge Uniserv contingent plus engineering corps from the developed nations launched the great pan-African water project: giant desalinizing plants built along both coasts, delivering fresh water through massive pipelines that ran through the new trans-Africa transportation corridor. Completed in 2049, the newly irrigated Africa became the central focus of the Climate Justice program,

When your father was growing up, UniServ recruits were assigned to African infrastructure improvement: smart cities, robotized logistics, decentralized electric microgrids, distributed telemedicine and more. For Dylan's generation, Africa was the place to be: a land of opportunity and growth, unlike the more limited horizons in the developed world.

He hoped for central Africa, but drew Sicily, and in the end, it changed his life as much as Texas did mine.

Dylan was stationed at a large airbase at Comiso, in the Iblean hills in southeastern Sicily, about 30 kilometers from where your mother grew up. Those hills were an ancient place, where first the Greeks and then the Romans settled. Much of their mythology was set there: Persephone was kidnapped, Bacchus discovered wine, Ulysses battled the Cyclops. And there were still monsters there a century ago: Comiso was the launching base for a fleet of American nuclear cruise missiles.

Dylan's job was supply line coordinator, managing the big hydrogen drones that ferried supplies from the base, outside the old Baroque town of Noto, to the frontline forces who were reforesting unused agricultural land. (I suspect that your father's aptitude tests indicated his skills would be better used sitting in a cool indoor space doing remote drone operation than chasing errant seedling bots down rugged Sicilian hillsides).

One of the goals in global reforestation is to return parts of the planet to historical conditions; in the case of Sicily, recreating some of the interior landscape before the Romans harvested the island's trees for construction and agriculture. Young trees absorb the most carbon; as your Sicilian grandfather used to tell his guests: "A hectare of olive trees removes 26 tons of carbon a year and gives us 8,000 liters of olive oil."

(In the US Midwest, we are still reforesting farmland that is no longer needed, thanks to precision agriculture and vertical farming. The goal was aboveground woody biomass approximating the early 1800s. In those days, they say, Ohio was so densely forested that a squirrel could travel from one side of the state to the other without ever touching the ground.)

Sicily still exported heritage wheat, fruit, and olives, but less land was needed for cultivation. Hence the reforestation. By the time your father arrived in 2070, some work was already done. But there were still large areas with extreme species imbalances and diseased ecosystems, remnants of the terrible fires that swept across much of southern Europe in the 2020s and 2030s, when the Warming was at its worst.

Early in the 2050s, the EU prioritized parts of inland Sicily for restoration as an analog zone. Analog zones are places that maintain some connection with the previrtual world, in customs, crafts, landscape, language, or culture. The analog zones were essentially the UNESCO World Heritage program of the previous century, but increased to encompass entire regions, including more areas in Africa, South and Central America and Asia.

Analog zone is a bit of a misnomer—there are still virtual services, so the zones aren't some sort of analog-cult retreat. Sicily, for example, has many small villages, once nearly deserted, that were revived and are now thriving due to virtualization. The original walkables, you could say.

* * *

In the two years since Marianna died, your father and I had grown very close. So when he left for UniServ, he worried that I might grow lonely, and insisted that we spend a bit of time together almost every day during his time in Sicily. Most days he would link me in his eyeline all afternoon, so I could drop in and sit with him as he worked.

In early July, he had some leave time, and decided to visit a nearby ancient Roman villa. It was an astonishingly well-preserved ruin, with intricate mosaic floors documenting a dozen moments in the country life of wealthy Romans. The mosaics were nearly as bright as if created in this century rather than 1,800 years ago.

Because the villa is so intact, it boasts one of the best Roman-era AR recreations in Europe. In general, the Europeans are very good at historical AR: realistic casting, costuming, not shy of nudity or mild violence when appropriate. American recreations tend to be more antiseptic;

we've always preferred to pretty our history up a bit. (Or a lot, depending on how bad the particular history was.)

The rush hour scene at Historic Suburb Park in Virginia, for example, is beautifully staged, with perfect period details, but the disputes between the drivers are too friendly. I know what car traffic was like in the 2020s, and if you didn't hear somebody shouting "Idiot!" or worse at the top of their lungs, and sounding their horn like an insane person, well, it wasn't really rush hour.

Anyway, your father knew that I'm a big fan of AR restorations, so he invited me to go along on the tour. He messaged me when he bought our tickets. It was six hours earlier in New Williamsburg so I quickly finished breakfast, put on some comfortable glasses, and stretched out on the couch.

Your father looped me into his eyeline as he climbed the external metal stairs to an elevated walkway that ran atop the walls of the ancient villa. We exchanged a few pleasantries and then the tour triggered when we reached the top step.

The tour had a great opening fade-in: the shattered walls rose up as if new. Elaborately painted ceilings materialized overhead, knitting together digitally to shut out the intense blue Sicilian sky.

Torches appeared on the stone walls, then squat wooden furniture, brightly painted, bulging cushions embroidered in reds and ochres. Then, below us, the Romans appeared—first, dark-skinned servants, lighting torches, then the noble family and their retainers. I am always struck in historically accurate ARs by how short humans once were!

Dylan and I walked around the elevated path above the

rooms, looking down on the scene. We could hear soft chattering in archaic Latin, then saw the servants working in the kitchen and laundry. A bit further along, we arrived at the lavish tiled baths, where two women of the house were being tended by three young enslaved girls.

It was somewhere around the baths that your father paused the restoration—I wasn't sure why; he's usually entranced by historical AR—and he glanced up in realview, across to the opposite wall of the baths. 30 or so meters away, on the facing walkway, another set of tourists were gathered, looking down at the bathers.

Among them was your mother, with long dark brown hair, large almond eyes, and a classically proportioned Roman face. She was looking straight across at us. When she saw that Dylan had noticed, she glanced away quickly.

I remember that moment well, although certainly not as well as your father does. He looked back down at the baths and we resumed viewing the restoration. The floor mosaic was a whimsical image of two young noblewomen wearing what appeared to be bikinis, tossing a colored ball between them.

"Really quite modern," I said softly to your father. "That could have come from the 20th century rather than the 3rd."

He continued to gaze in silence for a moment, and then paused the scene again. He glanced up and across the open room. Your mother was again looking over.

"She's beautiful," he said softly.

"I think you should go introduce yourself," I said. "I'll log off here."

And that is the day your father met your mother.

TIMESHIFTING

Timeshifting fascinates me, perhaps because my generation coasted along on the scientific breakthroughs of the 20th century for such a long time. It was the 1960s and the 1970s that brought us the first elements of the internet, personal computers, gene splicing. In the early days of the new century we were simply working out their obvious extensions.

I remember, in 2048, the public excitement over the first proof of quantum timeshifting. The event was a brief radio conversation between some European scientists and the team at the Brightside colony on the moon.

The words were simple: "Brightside, are you there?"

"Affirmative, Berlin."

What was remarkable about that conversation was that there was no time gap between the two sentences. In the past, there would have been two and a half seconds of unavoidable silence, the time it took for the question to arrive on the moon and the answer to return to earth, even traveling at the speed of light.

Timeshifting was discovered during experiments to increase the memory capacity of quantum computer chips. It turned out, for reasons not yet understood, that two electrons can occupy the same physical space by existing in different times, one in the present, one slightly in the past or future.

The Berlin-Brightside experiment created a great deal of excitement about timeshifting. As well as protestors and government hearings. "The biggest threat since nuclear weapons" is one phrase I recall.

The fear was that timeshifting would ultimately permit some mission into the past that would accidentally produce "forward ripples," catastrophic alterations in history. There was a well-worn science fiction plot in which the main character goes back in time and, for example, accidentally kills their own grandfather, so the character instantly ceases to exist in the present.

A global conference in Geneva drafted guidelines for safe timeshifting research. The Temporal Research Treaty stipulates that timeshifting experiments may not interfere with historical processes or exchange information. Timeshifting may not be used for any kind of speculative investing, whether sports betting or the stock market. And all timeshifting chips, which are still very expensive, must be registered with the government.

Tens of thousands of scientists work in temporal research labs. What is the theoretical basis of quantum time-shifting? How else can we use it? And if we do develop enhanced time travel, what are its hazards?

No one is quite certain whether quantum time-shifting is a unique case limited to electrons, or the beginning of a fundamental new tool. For now, we still can't timeshift anything more substantial than a stream of electrons.

Which is probably more exciting if you're an electron.

October 17, 2084

I turned 75 today. I tend not to observe my birthdays; I've never quite understood why one celebrates another year's accumulation of mileage. But your father insisted, and so we all went to a popular New Williamsburg restaurant for an early dinner. Your parents have already taken you there; I recall that you like watching the kitchen, and also have a favorite milkshake. I expect that heavily influenced their choice of dining establishment.

The restaurant is very stylized in an old-fashioned early century look—communal dining tables, antique neon tubing, exposed brick, wood accents, leafy plants dangling in the corners. I have no idea why this nostalgic theme has suddenly reemerged in the 2080s, since it was already nostalgia in my youth. But then these days there are many things I don't understand.

I am surprised to see there is even a nostalgic dish on the menu: an animal meat "flank steak." I wondered: is this a trend?

"It comes and goes," Dylan said. "I think every generation wants to taste animal meat at some point. If they can afford it."

I reminded him of the steak he had when we visited Texas, 25 years ago. "I'm still paying that off," I said, "and you didn't even finish it."

Dylan shook his head and smiled in your direction. "Kids. What can you do?"

You like the restaurant because it has an open design so you can see the entire kitchen. Like most central prep kitchens, it is mostly robotized, with preppers and tenders, chopbots, runners, service avatars, and so forth. There is a human chef in the kitchen, supervising, and since it's a big restaurant, two human hosts in the dining room.

You spent most of our meal watching the bots in the kitchen. They were programmed to be productive yet showy, with a series of antics like juggling eggs, or a sous chef that twirled knives like an old-time cowboy's revolvers. You particularly liked a rather unnecessary minidrone that kept swooping around doing odd jobs.

Ironically, my favorite restaurant when I was twelve or so was a hamburger joint near Times Square. It had opened after COVID and featured a hamburger-making robot. Cookbots were new then, and the restaurant had a big glass wall so you could watch the automated assembly line as it broke up lettuce heads, sliced buns and tomatoes, even ground the meat for every order. I still remember you could order a mix of real beef and buffalo meat.

I loved it, but our visits there ended when my parents, very progressive in their politics, saw one of the restaurant owners say on television that as manufacturing costs dropped, within a few years burgerbots would be cheaper to use than humans.

AUTOMATION

Post-COVID, all industries accelerated automation. Given a choice between rehiring workers or buying machines and software, the corporate powers didn't hesitate. Robots and software didn't get sick, needed no sleep and never grew disgruntled or demanding. Machinery could be depreciated on your taxes, and by the time you needed to replace a bot, the new model was better and cheaper.

Humans were the most expensive and least reliable aspect of almost every business. AI and automation steadily eliminated jobs, from strawberry pickers to hamburger cooks to junior accountants to young lawyers to street sweepers to truck drivers and millions upon millions of "vice-presidents," all replaced with various kinds of bots, from intelligent software to autonomous vehicles.

At first, since we were coming back from record unemployment, the impact on job numbers wasn't immediately obvious. Jobs became increasingly contingent and precarious: month-to-month, week-to-week, even hour-to-hour. Human schedules were driven by software rather than people. At the same time, corporate profits continued to grow.

If you owned robots and software, automation didn't look like a problem. Corporate interests spent millions on think-tank research proving that automation and artificial intelligence would eliminate boring low-paid work and replace it with compelling and lucrative new jobs.

"New jobs" was an important argument for the corporate powers to advance, since in the early century, cities and states competed relentlessly to offer the biggest tax credits to attract factories and offices and warehouses. If you were an enormous etailer asking for $100 million in tax breaks to build a warehouse in Kansas, the last thing you wanted to say was that within a decade you planned to fill that warehouse with robots and software that would stock shelves and fill orders 24 hours a day with only a handful of humans in sight.

Economists were paid to explain jobs losses away: seasonal variability, secular weakness, inventory backlogs. It was similar to the way that in the early century, American politicians would point to heavy snowfall as proof there was no Warming. Shareholder value thrived on misdirection.

The corporatist cheerleaders also liked to say that we simply needed to invent new jobs, and that humans just needed to learn new skills and try harder. It was another misdirection: blame the unemployed. Many of these now-obsolete service jobs had been called "essential" just a few years earlier during COVID.

There were still good and important jobs to be done. The problem was that in the shareholder value model there was no one to pay the salaries.

That won't make any sense to you, so let me use an early-century example. A group of law graduates sued their law schools for promising them lucrative employment, when in fact by the 2020s, law firms were already automating much of the routine work usually given to new hires. There simply weren't as many secure, well-paying jobs for young lawyers.

The law students lost their case. As I recall, the judge said that if they were smart enough to go to law school they were smart enough to know there weren't many jobs. Again, blame the unemployed.

But here's the irony: in fact, there were many jobs for young lawyers, as public defenders. During the American mass incarceration era, thousands of often innocent citizens remained in cells due to a lack of legal representation. But there was little funding to hire public defenders. And so it was for many other jobs in social services and childcare and education, not to mention the arts and culture.

Ironically, full automation, this last spasm of corporate greed, ultimately benefited us all. "Maximizing shareholder value" was a ruthless and pitiless driver of increased automation, allowing no sentimentality, no nostalgia, no ethical hesitation in removing human labor from the world of work. Yet in the end it was those massive investments that created the robot workforce that now pays everyone Living Income while freeing us to do more valuable work.

Tuesday. October 24

A few days ago, I spent an hour sitting at the Chardinist chapel, about a five-minute walk from my building. Since Marianna's death I sometimes stroll over just to sit in the quiet space. Priest Anne was there, in a front pew, talking to a parishioner. She's in her fifties, very kind, and knew your grandmother Marianna well. I was never a regular attendee, but she always recognizes me. I promised Dylan I'd talk to Anne, but for now I just wanted some quiet moments.

You've been to the Chardinist chapel a few times; it's the practice your father follows. Your mother more or less goes along with it. Like your grandmother, Sofia was raised as a Catholic. But she's a modern Italian Catholic; they tend to be very definitive about their faith but not necessarily so observant.

I love the quiet interior, high-ceilinged and spare, with the soft sound of running water. There's a realistic woodland stream that emerges from the back wall, meanders along one side of the room, and disappears into the back wall, just to one side of the altar. The stream has natural maintenance; along both banks are water lilies, some perennial grasses, and my favorite, the swamp hibiscus.

As I was about to leave, the priest came over. We made a bit of small talk about the weather; she asked how you were doing and I told her my guess that you're going to be in Space Club.

She was silent for a moment and then cleared her throat. "Do you mind if I ask: Do you see upholding as a way to be reunited with Marianna?"

I was surprised by the question. "What makes you ask that?"

"Dylan talked to me about it. He and Sofia are very concerned."

"Well," I said, "I don't know that I see it that way."

"May I sit with you?" the priest asked.

Anne joined me in the smooth hickory pew and looked at me for a moment. "We don't believe that preserving the connectome is a reason to curtail a vital natural life, either analog or virtual."

"Well, I wouldn't do it until it was absolutely necessary."

"What about my first question? Do you think upholding might reconnect you with Marianna?"

At first, I said no, I know perfectly well that when a mind is upheld, it doesn't lead to a virtual afterlife. There's no indication that the many thousands of connectomes currently in storage worldwide are active in any way.

Or perhaps that's just my rational mind. I mean, we really don't know what happens when connectomes are entwined with Nous. After all, there is that mysterious electrical current flow between stored connectomes that no one has really explained. Is there more experience that I can someday share with Marianna?

"You do know," asked Anne, "that upholding is not part of Church doctrine?"

"Of course. Marianna and I discussed that years ago."

"The goal of evolution, the Omega Point, doesn't represent resurrection. It's a culmination. It's a single immortal, collective intelligence that will outlive the heat death of the universe, and then create the next universe. But it's neither heaven nor resurrection in the old Christian sense."

"Well, you have to admit, life in heaven, reuniting with

your loved ones, is a pretty attractive concept."

"Heaven was a useful and soothing metaphor for a long time. Now we'd say that Marianna is already woven into the fabric of Nous. As you will be, and I, and everyone we know. One thing we try to do in Chapel is to be still enough to hear a bit of those familiar voices. And to learn to sense their presence everywhere in the world."

I smiled. Priest Anne was very kind, but I know a sales pitch when I hear one. "Thank you," I said. "Always good to talk with you."

FAMILY HISTORY;
NEW WILLIAMSBURG 2055

Marianna and I came from very different backgrounds, but we seemed to understand each other right away. We had the same sense of the absurd—we'd both see something strange or off-putting or unexpected and look at each other and start laughing. It was a very good way of coping with a world that, especially in the tumult of the 2030s and 2040s, could be strange and unexpected and off-putting, often all at the same time.

When I think of that, I always remember your father's pusspup. Maybe he's already told you about little Boson.

When Dylan was five, he decided that he wanted to adopt a rather sad creature called a pusspup. "Pusspup" was a character in one of his favorite video games, and a Chinese biotech company had created a line of actual pusspup clones as a tie-in. Novelty clones were illegal in the US, following the international rules on responsible genetic engineering, but the Chinese were still creating them for their domestic market.

Somehow an illegal shipment of pusspups ended up at

a puppy farm outside Columbus. Neighbors reported the odd-looking animals and the farm was shut down. That left about 300 young pusspups stranded in Ohio, through no fault of their own. After some back-and-forth with the courts and animal rights groups, they were put up for compassionate adoption.

Your grandmother and I were in our early 40s then, and we were immediately against the idea. We simply weren't a generation that grew up with modified mammals. But one of the dilemmas of growing older in a rapidly changing world is trying to decide when you're defending basic human values, and when you're simply being an old fogey.

This time we erred on the side of avoiding fogey-hood. We adopted. Dylan immediately took little Boson, as he named him, to his best friend's house. The mother, who was about our age, dropped a plate and screamed: "Get that thing out of here this instant!" Not a good start.

The pusspup was not a true chimera; it was more a dog with some cat-like features. I suppose the idea, besides the game tie-in, was that you received the affection and trainability of a dog with the esthetics of a cat. But it was not a practical pet—most troubling was the fact that natural cats and dogs, even the most peaceful, attacked pusspups whenever they encountered them.

Your father loved little Boson, but pusspups did not catch on. Even in China, the fad only lasted a year or so, which, sadly, turned out to be the lifespan of the little clones themselves.

Ultimately, there was some beneficial feline reengineering: British researchers suppressed the hunting reflex in the domestic house cat, reducing songbird fatalities by hundreds of millions a year. So perhaps Boson's short life was not altogether in vain, at least from the point of view of the average chickadee.

The only thing that lasted at our house was the phrase "pusspup."

Marianna and I began using that to describe any fad or fashion or bit of gadgetry that looked loony and we'd both start laughing immediately.

MAKING BABIES

In the early century, futurists said we would soon be creating designer babies—that human genetic engineering would let us become a different species, taller, smarter, stronger.

It hasn't quite worked out that way. Genetic modifications are all around us, from housecats and grapevines to the production cells in a poultry bioreactor. We can treat hundreds of genetic disorders, and mediate many of what were once called diseases of civilization, from obesity to depression. But there are still many mysteries remaining about humans.

Creative intelligence, courage, curiosity, empathy and more—we don't really understand how these arise. Even simpler traits, like hair color or height, are complicated enough genetically that to wade in and start moving around gene sequences is still too unpredictable. It's a form of surgery, and just as with neural implants, a good result isn't guaranteed.

Tragic stories emerged from the 2030s intelligence augmentation projects in China and Eastern Europe—those oddly twisted children, the blurry genetic line between genius and deep autism, the so-called Jakarta Manimal who lived for a full decade hidden in an Indonesian slum—all testimony to what we do not yet know. We don't fully comprehend the interaction of environment, experience, and society that creates a human mind. It is the ultimate unquantifiable.

Your father's generation was among the last to have randomly-selected genomes. Although Marianna and I were cautious: we had our full geneprints run through hypothetical embryo generation, which creates and analyzes thousands of potential recombinations.

On the basis of our hypotheticals, the counselor said we wouldn't need IVF and embryo screening, unless we ran into fertility issues. Egg harvesting back then was still an arduous process for women.

So we rolled our genetic dice and your father turned out rather well, if I do say so myself.

Now it's different. Five years after Dylan was born, in vitro gametogenesis was finally approved for standard conception, which lets doctors create both eggs and sperm from the parents' stem cells. (IVG had been permitted earlier only for infertile and same-sex couples, and was often not productive). The current practice is to create about five thousand eggs. Combined with either natural or IVG sperm, that yields at least 1,000 healthy zygotes to scan for optimal recombinations.

In the developed world, a majority of people opt for IVG and preimplant zygote scans. Gene surgery to modify embryos is rare and risky. It's only attempted when the DNA of the parents can't produce an embryo without serious single-gene defects.

One early century fear about preselection hasn't come to pass: male-female choice ends up at about the naturally occurring 1:1 ratio, due to high gender equality in most societies. Except in a few nations that retain less-evolved gender roles, parents derive no particular social or economic benefit from either choice.

FAMILY HISTORY:
TEXAS - NEW WILLIAMSBURG 2034

As was often the case for my generation, I found an occupation during my UniServ posting at the Texas carbon plant. Officially I was assigned to the kitchen and last-mile traffic control, but my second year of service I made friends with a mechanic who repaired onsite robotics: the automated fork-lifts, kitchen robots, crew transports, support drones and so forth. On my time off I'd tag along with him, and something about the combination of software and mechanical parts made sense to me. I had a knack for simple programming but didn't want to sit in a room all day; I wanted to work with my hands.

When Marianna and I finished service and moved to New Williamsburg I used my ed creds for a one-year mechatronics program in Columbus. That's how your nonno Aldus became a robot repairman.

One way or another, robots looked like the future to me, and it has been a steady job for nearly fifty years. As it turns out, robots are very good at building robots, but they're not that good at *fixing* robots.

I hoped for an exciting job. Oceanic robot repair, for example. In the mid-2030s, that was adventure: the world was beginning to launch the tiny millipede coral cultivators and the pelagic plastic collectors and the gawky swimming robots that service the offshore wind farms. But Ohio is far from the nearest ocean, and I wasn't about to move again. Sea-going mechatronics was not in my future.

Instead, I ended up doing something far less exotic: nursing home robotics. Back then, in the US, many Boomers and Gen Xers were growing old and frail, often without sufficient pensions or savings. Quite a few senior facilities had gone bankrupt after COVID, and senior housing was always drastically underfunded. The corporate powers were still dominant, so the Federal government created a shareholder-friendly program: corporations received huge government subsidies to build low-cost for-profit senior housing across the US.

So my first job was as a robotics tech for Consolidated Comfort, a company headquartered in Columbus. CC had huge amounts of private equity money behind it, and for years had been buying up senior housing all around the US.

Senior housing was an easy target for automation. The buildings were, by law, fully accessible, from wheelchair ramps to wide doors and lever doorknobs. By happy (at least for CC) coincidence, that also made them extremely robot-friendly.

When CC bought a senior home, they would lay off most of the workers and automate. They installed bots for many jobs—kitchen, laundry, meal distribution, patient monitoring. Beacons were built into the halls so bots could navigate easily. The rooms were designed to be cleaned by bots, the beds had machine-changeable linens, the rooms were festooned with health sensors, and everything was networked and managed with an AI dashboard to maximize efficiency.

Each facility was actually one huge intelligent machine for keeping old people alive and reasonably comfortable.

I have to admit, I had some hesitation about the Consolidated Comfort job. In the mid-2030s, protests against automation were growing more radical in the US. It was at the height of the labor troubles—the Work for All movement, which ultimately led to both Fair Work and Living Income, a happy conclusion after much pain.

But Marianna and I were newlyweds, just starting out, and she still had at least three years of college ahead of her.

I'd been on the job less than a year before I was caught, rather painfully, in the middle of a protest action. I was sent to Kansas City for a few weeks, overseeing the automation of a newly-acquired senior home, when an underground protest collective called SaBotage targeted Consolidated Comfort for an action.

SaBotage was one of the last large protest organizations. There were quite a few unemployed computer programmers at the time; much of their work had been automated by AI as well. Other lower-level IT workers had been replaced by bots tending the giant cloud server farms. The result was many smart, angry young technologists, who supported the movement against unregulated automation by developing sophisticated jamming tools to disrupt robots at a distance.

I have a collection of bot-killers in a jar on my desk, souvenirs of the bad old days. The sabotage devices were clever little hacks: plastic cylinders or disks the size of lipsticks or matchboxes, that could be smuggled into factories or restaurants or warehouses to jam bot communications.

In Kansas City, there was a bot-killer I didn't find in time. I was testing a patient lifter, a very new robot that used a bulky assembly of soft rubber and silicone arms to move seniors from beds to wheelchairs. It was needed because in the early century, many elderly were extremely large, sometimes several hundred kilos; back then, corporate food was engineered to be cheap and addictive.

I was alone when I tested the lifter on myself. That was a violation of safety rules; I shouldn't have tried it without an assistant. I laid back, activated the bot and its smooth silicone arms slid under me gently, then started to lift me out of the bed. But suddenly the bot bucked and threw me into the air. I broke my right hand cushioning my fall to the floor; the wrist joint still clicks when I turn it just so.

Later it turned out that a maintenance worker, about to be laid off, had slipped a SaBotage device under the mattress. Sabotage was, of course, very illegal, and a half-dozen members ultimately went to jail.

The injury didn't turn me against Work for All. Quite the opposite:. I started to feel guilty about what we were doing at Consolidated. Workers—immigrants or the less educated—were being eliminated from the kitchens, dayrooms, laundries, and hallways. Management always promised that they would be retrained and rehired as individual caregivers. That, of course, rarely happened—shareholder value, after all.

I had seen a dozen fully automated senior homes with only a handful of human workers. The tiny bedrooms were filled with elderly residents having sad, circular conversations with companion robots, bizarre confections called elderbots, covered with synthetic fur that looked vaguely like seals, or plump puppies, or feline puffballs.

It was the same story as those unemployed young lawyers decades earlier: There were still important jobs to do, such as tending elders, but in the old system there was no one willing to pay to have it done properly. By the early 2040s, the passage of the Fair Work Act and Living Income meant there could be a vast expansion in socially valuable jobs with decent salaries, from eldercare to education, from counseling to childcare.

As my wrist was healing, I quit Consolidated Care and volunteered part-time in the Work for All movement, which grew increasingly powerful during the late 2030s.

We won. A few years ago, I visited an old pal from my Texas UniServ years, who happened to be in an eldercare facility. I was pleased to see that the halls of the home were filled with bots to do the physical work—as well as plenty of well-trained humans to provide care and companionship.

WORK

Early-century films and novels about working life may sometimes make little sense to you. When I was young, people often had jobs they disliked intensely, jobs performed only for money, jobs that made a thriving family life difficult. Many basic jobs were divided into little units, parceled out by AIs to people who could no longer afford to say no. In the US, if someone lost a job, they could quickly face homelessness, food shortage, compromised health. Work was literally life and death for many.

By the late 2020s, young people of all educational levels were underemployed, or had become at-home pieceworkers, with few prospects or stability. In a final humiliation the corporate media exhorted us to develop our "brands," as if we were products rather than people.

And the nation itself grew richer and richer.

Richer, that is, for some. The main financial measurement in the early century was a number called Gross Domestic Product. The GDP of a nation, however, often bore little resemblance to the individual wellness of its citizens. As a famous politician named Robert Kennedy said over a century ago: "GDP measures everything except that which makes life worthwhile." (He was assassinated 3 months after he said that.)

After the Second Constitutional Congress in the United States, economists created a new measure of national wealth, called Per Capita Wellness—incorporating water, food, shelter, safety, and health. Perhaps we needed a "gross" number a century ago, when measuring tools were crude. But now it's easy to pull PCW data from all of the country's various data feeds—including individual information like one's Double. It's voluntary, of course, whether you contribute personal data to the PCW survey, although 95% of the US population does.

(The data are also compiled on a local basis. New Williamsburg has always been in the top 10% of municipal PCWs).

Once the hidden wealth of the ultrarich and the corporations was opened up, it was clear that even with the costs of fighting the Warming, we as a species were far richer than we'd thought in the early century. The result of that was Living Income, a flat guaranteed income for every adult.

It has taken decades, dollar by dollar, but now every individual over 18 receives enough Living Income for a healthy and comfortable life. There is also of course, a child allowance.

The Living Income fund grew in large part due to automation. As robots filled our factories and farms and distribution networks, the money saved on labor costs went into Living Income. We all profited each time there was an advance in automation. Some people called it the Gates tax—many years ago the philanthropist Bill Gates suggested a "robot tax"—but of course the computation is much more complicated than counting robots.

Living Income is not what was once called socialism; what has evolved is a market economy based on sharing principles. Arriving at this model was not an easy process. Early in our history, the stronger members of our species invented hierarchical social systems in which those with temporary advantages could sustain and multiply their privilege for generations. Humans have had kings and queens and land barons and feudal lords and corporate oligarchs for so long that we'd forgotten these roles were not innate.

Well into the middle of the 21st century, China and Russia harbored the largest remnants of the ultrarich aristocracies, long after the rest of the developed world had moved to sharing. The irony, you will learn, is that these two countries were the bastions of failed attempts at an early sharing economy called Communism. So why did they remain the last redoubts of stratified class systems in this century?

One theory is that both nations experimented with ideas of sharing long before there was sufficient technology to run a true sharing economy. How could a vast nation plan and manage sharing without the realtime data we now have from millions of sensors and satellites, and the AI to interpret and formulate distribution?

In the last century it proved impossible. Communism had other structural flaws as well, so very quickly both nations collapsed into corrupt authoritarian cronyism, deeply tainting their collective memories about sharing. The 20th-century failures of China and Russia, from mass starvation to systemic murder, provided cautionary tales that the ultrarich regularly used in the US to inspire fear, whenever the less fortunate questioned shareholder-value capitalism.

Another dire corporate warning we heard in the early century was that with a guaranteed income, people would no longer want to work. But that is not the case. Most everyone *does* work at something, and there is a job for everyone. Exactly as it was for early humans: in the ancestral environment, everyone in the tribe or camp or village had a role. Idlers were rare, and usually possessed some underlying disorder.

Humans are social creatures and once one strips away the artifice of occupational "status," we are fulfilled by contributing to others, in service, care, craft, or art. A main goal of the educational system and the lifelong relationship with Tutor is to ensure that every student finds proper employment.

Work is also more evenly distributed. In the early century, some people did not have enough work and others worked sixty or seventy hours a week. LI meant a shorter workweek. Half of the week is devoted to work; the other half is weekend. Many of us work longer hours, because we wish to, or have occupations in which hours are difficult to control.

Weekend, by the way, used to mean Saturday and Sunday. The fixed weekend started to decline during the War, as a way to evenly manage resource consumption. Now, floating weekends are common in most jobs; my weekend was usually Tuesday, Wednesday and Thursday morning.

Unless you are working all-volunteer, you'll earn a salary

on top of LI. And people such as high-responsibility managers or successful entrepreneurs and entertainers may have a much higher earned income (and no LI, of course, after a certain level).

Some people do very well. There is the popular singer, Vanja Klein, who performs corny old songs and rhymes from the 2030s and 2040s, like "Snow in September" or "UniServ-i-T." Her wardrobes are expensive—she appeared recently in a gown of engineered phosphorescent algae, millions of tiny creatures growing on a form-fitting fabric substrate. Vanja looked like a glowing nude hallucination—a look achieved through analog methods. Gen Z audiences love wartime nostalgia.

There are also people with management jobs of great responsibility who are well-rewarded, although their total salaries can't exceed 20 times that of their average employee (in the early century, corporate CEOs earned hundreds of times more than their employees). Salaries are based on a combination of responsibility plus contribution to per capital wellness.

An example from my generation is the much-beloved Kesha Adams, now in her early 80s, CEO since the mid-2050s of the largest food intelligence network across the Americas and Canada.

She oversees thousands of workers who operate the food surveillance network, tracking fresh produce, bioengineered foods, prepared meals—all of our nutrition—making sure that distribution is safe, efficient, and minimizes waste.

Kesha has several houses around the world. She's rich enough that after she won her first Orbital award, she paid with her own money to go back up two more times. But she also pays a great deal in taxes.

Or there's Steven Valdez, a geneticist who worked on the US ocean reforestation project for years. When he was 40, he left the service to start a company with his domestic partner, a clothing designer. They've made kelp leather jackets, quite stylish and comfortable, for twenty years now. (In my opinion, there are too many Valdez Kelps walking around town these days, but it's fashion so what can you do?)

I've seen pictures of the Valdez house in Kauai and it's an amazing piece of architecture, threading through a restored pre-European forest, most of it open to the public.

FAMILY HISTORY:
NEW WILLIAMSBURG, 2060

Like many of my contemporaries, I more or less stumbled into finding a job that I liked. Your father found his profession the same way you will: through thoughtful consideration by both Tutor and humans.

Early on in your father's education it grew clear that, like me, he did not have what is colloquially called "the reading gene." Not that there is a single gene for reading, just as there are no simple genomics for anything worthwhile in human nature.

Reading is a very recent evolutionary development, and an unnatural skill in terms of our ancestral needs. Now with so many alternative ways to communicate there's no reason to stigmatize those without the inborn knack for letters.

My generation was the last expected to be able to fluently write freehand. It is different for your father's generation, raised with autoparsers. (The Europeans remain fond of freehand writing. Your mother is bilingual, Italian and English, and I don't think she uses an autoparser for either. Local language is still prized by many Europeans, protected, and considered as much as a part of the natural landscape as trees or rivers.)

In the US, any student with native writing aptitude is identified early on by Tutor and specifically schooled to create prose without an autoparser. It's a little like identifying natural athletes. Fluency is a great talent, and I still love to spend an evening listening to a pair of prose artists improvise in freehand English. And there is a lively audience of readers for documents of all lengths, on topics both educational and narrative. But reading is neither everyone's taste nor skill.

Once I suggested that your father switch off his autoparser. He was quick to remind me that when I was young we used all kinds of fancy fonts on our computers that none of us could reproduce by hand.

He had a point. In fact, for many centuries, there was a handwriting technique specifically designed to speed a pen's passage over paper. But no longer. In the early century, cursive writing gradually disappeared from school curricula.

Dylan's difficulty with words might well have doomed his educational progress in generations past. Not today. While Tutor William worked patiently to improve your father's writing and reading, he also relied heavily on audio and video and simulations to teach your father about the world.

Dylan's interest level was always highest when he put on haptic gloves and did virtual chemistry experiments. At first we thought it was the usual juvenile male fascination with triggering explosions. (That's a benefit of virtual study; in my high school chem lab, explosions were strongly discouraged.)

Your father's math skills were also high, and when he was 12 or so, Tutor introduced him to some chemists and material scientists who talked about their work. One of them was from the Chrysopeia Materials Lab, a large research campus a bit south of New Williamsburg. As soon as your father heard the story about their synthetic gold ingot, he wanted to visit in person.

Dylan's teacher was a bright young man named Akram, and when we next met, I expressed some surprise that Dylan was interested in material science; it seemed rather drab compared to biotech or robots.

Akram politely indicated that I was showing my age. "That may have been true when you were young. But if I was Dylan's age, with his inclinations, the two most exciting areas are matter synthesis and timeshifting. Tutor William and I have talked about this quite a bit. For now, timeshifting is mostly software and math, and Dylan is more focused on physical science."

Your father was a highly distractible child at the time, and I thought it awfully early to be talking about a 10-year-old's career path. But as it turned out, Tutor and teacher saw something not obvious even to Dylan's own father.

MATERIAL WORLD

Suppose someone from the earlier years of the 20th century was suddenly transported fifty years into the future. What would most amaze them about 1975?

One might logically guess television, or perhaps airplanes. But our theoretical time travelers had already seen an airplane. And they'd quickly figure out that television was just radio with pictures.

In 1975, one object that might be most amazing is the transparent plastic bag—because that would have been impossible to make with any known material in 1925. Materials change the world.

On the other hand, those changes aren't always for the better. It took about 10,000 giant pelagic trashbots two decades to clear the plastic debris in the oceans. On land, countless injections of plastic-digesting bacteria into abandoned trash-dumps. Then, all the bacteria had to be eliminated by triggering their suicide genes. Quite a fuss, all in all. Your father likes to say that we should always ask whether today's science is producing next century's plastic pollution.

In the late 2030s, the Chrysopoeia lab led the research in the synthesis of rare materials and minerals—substances previously obtained by mining the planet. One summer day in 2045, the lab made international news by creating a one kilogram bar of artificial gold, proof that they had mastered "low-temperature non-nuclear metal synthesis."

The gold bar (stamped with the old alchemist's phrase *Chrysopoeia*) had been worth $100,000 the day before the lab's press conference; the day after, it was worth a tenth of that. And within a few years the lab would be able to create a kilogram of gold for about $30.

Synthetic gold was not unexpected and most of the world's financial systems had already been weaned off gold as a unit of value. But that wooded lab in Ohio did put an end to the 21st century's last grand private space project: asteroid mining.

A consortium of ultrarich, mostly in China and Russia, were funding plans to send spacecraft to mine asteroids. The idea was to extract rare minerals from the asteroid belt or the surface of the moon, and then ferry the riches back to earth. The extractive industries, a destructive human specialty for thousands of years, were about to be exported to space.

However, after creating gold, the Materials Lab, now renamed Chrysopoeia Lab, quickly synthesized a half-dozen "rare earths," substances crucial to modern electronics and energy storage. Mined in only a few countries, rare earths had been powerful economic weapons in 21st century geopolitics.

Today, we have synthetic replacements for the rare earths, as well as more common metals. Copper and iron, once destined to be exhausted in this century, are now usually replaced with carbon-based synthetics that are stronger, or more conductive, or more flexible than the originals.

The synthesis of rare metals and minerals meant an end to the asteroid mining venture. A Wild West mining expedition 500,000,000 kilometers into space no longer made economic sense.

Ironically, at the same time, the breakthroughs in material science led to the Space Elevator project in the 2050s, and a complete transformation of how we travel into space.

FAMILY HISTORY:
CHRYSOPOEIA LABS, 2062

Your father was 12 when we visited Chrysopoeia. It's a beautiful campus where about two thousand researchers work, spread across eight hectares of restored native woodland: box elders, black walnut, birch, and magnolia. First, of course, we had to stop and see the original synthetic gold ingot, on display in the reception area. It was in a simple vitrine, beautifully lit, with holograms of the original press event back in 2045. The ingot was intentionally unpolished, even a bit dull.

Your father was fascinated; he'd just studied this bit of history with Tutor. I found it anticlimactic. Gold had glittered brighter when it still cost a thousand dollars an ounce. It was sad to think of the wars fought, the millions of lives lost, seizing or defending bits of this stolid metal.

Actually, for your father, the high point of the trip was seeing the researchers in one of the Lab's Common Rooms. He'd never before seen so large an ambient telepresence room, and I could tell it caught his imagination.

The Common Room was a large, airy open space, done

in white with calm pastel accents. It had blond wood tables, chairs, and couches in various conversational configurations, all on silicone sliders for easy rearrangement. On the wall where we entered there was a small snack bar, with food and drinks and two waitbots to keep all in order. A dozen or so researchers were seated in various areas around the Common Room. None particularly noticed us; they were clearly accustomed to passing tours.

At first glance, the Common Room looked much larger than it really was. On three sides there were huge active walls, each opening onto an identical Common Room: one out in California at Stanford, one in Tokyo, and one in Frankfurt. Each had the same color floor and walls; the same tables, chairs, and couches, so the Common Room in Columbus merged almost invisibly with the other three to create the sense of a single, very spacious room. I had never seen such a beautifully crafted ambient telepresence space before; Chrysopoeia clearly treated its researchers well.

It was about noon, so to my right, a dozen Stanford researchers through one wall were having morning coffees and pastries. In Frankfurt it was past six, so steins of beer and plates of cheese were in evidence. And though it was after midnight in Tokyo, there were still four young researchers in their semi-darkened Common Room—three of them stretched out on couches sound asleep.

"Listen," I told Dylan. We could hear someone from Stanford talking, just to our right. Several of the Ohio researchers near us had pulled up chairs to sit in a small group with their California colleagues. They were also wearing glasses and gesturing in the air, reviewing documents, planning the next steps at Stanford, based on that morning's work at Chrysopoeia.

In another corner of the room, a cluster of chairs included two Germans, two Ohio researchers and three from Stanford. Of course, the same conversations would take place eight or ten hours later, this time between Stanford and Tokyo. And Ohio, if anyone here was still awake.

Twenty-four hour workdays that circle the globe are not uncommon in science, because often all the labs are sharing the same piece of equipment, satellite, or observatory. A single experimental matter-synthesis foundry takes up half a city block, costs billions of dollars, and is shared virtually by a dozen or so material science labs around the world.

In fact, by coincidence, the biggest American matter foundry is in west Texas, not far from where your grandmother and I met fifty years ago. The solar panel array we helped build for the decarbonization plant is still one of the largest in the country, so the foundry can tap almost unlimited amounts of energy.

After we left Chrysopoeia that day, while we were waiting for the shuttle outside the gates, your father announced that next he wanted to go visit the Pecos matter foundry.

"We'll see if you're still interested in another few years," I told him.

"Oh," your father said, with the serene confidence of a precocious twelve-year-old, "I will be."

* * *

Four years later, we visited the Pecos foundry. But first we made a side trip to the site of Arrhenius, the giant carbon sequestration plant where Marianna and I had worked so many years ago.

The plant had closed five years earlier, with a ceremony that celebrated the success of the carbon drawdown. There was now a tall monument, made of carbon-sequestered stone, and we took a nice VR tour that captured the plant's operation in its prime.

In analog, the grounds had been naturalized and native prairie grasses covered the site. But if you looked carefully, you could still see some of the building footprints. "There," I told Dylan, pointing to a barely visible rectangle, dotted with desert brush. "That's where I met your mother."

In retrospect it was probably an underwhelming sight, but your father was patient, at least for a 16-year-old, and pretended he actually saw something.

After the Pecos tour, there was one other tourist stop we couldn't miss: the Permian Basin Historical Monument in Texas, a beautifully-detailed oilfield restoration with an excellent VR tour. You could buy little sealed bottles of actual crude oil in the gift shop, and I believe your father still has it on his desk.

We returned home and your father redoubled his studies. Tutor shifted to a learning path more oriented to the physical sciences. Your father had already decided he wanted to study at Stanford's Materials Lab at the Toronto campus.

The Silicon Valley earthquake in 2032 fatally shook investor confidence and put an emphatic end to what had once been an almost mythical center of technical innovation, fueled by a relentless financial machine. Nowadays the Valley has returned to its predigital state. The apricot and cherry orchards are beautiful in the spring.

Much of the high-tech exodus from Silicon Valley ended up in Canada, which in the early century had a far more stable government than the US, as well as tax incentives for new companies and a surprise membership in the European Economic Area. Not to mention improving weather.

I visited your father several times while he was studying in Toronto. Stanford Toronto lacks the historical resonance of the legacy campus in Silicon Valley, but has far more advanced infrastructure. And the weather in Toronto has certainly improved in the 60 years since my parents took me there for a memorably cold vacation.

Your father did extremely well at Stanford, and now he's a senior research director at Chrysopoeia. So I suspect you'll soon see that aging gold ingot for yourself.

MEAT

Your father had one other memorable experience when we visited the Pecos foundry back in 2056: He tasted his first animal meat, at a small restaurant on the road back to El Paso, one of those little boutique places that caters to carnivores. As I recall, Dylan chose a well-done sirloin steak, and he ate two bites and shook his head.

"It's not like I thought it would be," he said. I ordered barbecued brisket for us instead, from the non-animal side of the menu. It was excellent, and born and raised in a bioreactor.

I was vegan when I was young, and was happily surprised by how quickly synthetic meat became popular. Gen Z was probably the first to turn to synthetic meat in significant numbers, initially in the US and Europe. By the late 2020s, there were numerous decent substitutes for meat, and most popular restaurants served a few synthetics.

Soon synthetics spread to the developing world—another surprise. In the 2020s, before the Strike and the War, we feared that the growing global middle class would consume vast quantities of meat. And mass meat farming was an environmental disaster, from pollution and greenhouse gas to excessive water and land usage.

Once again, however, the corporate world proved useful. Synthetic meat marketers borrowed an idea from the previous century's promotion of another, less healthy product: baby formula. In the mid-20th century, the corporate powers sold baby formula to the Third World as the modern alternative to breast milk, implying that mothers might harm their babies by clinging to the old ways. As was often the case with corporate messaging, it was an exaggeration in the service of commerce.

In a similar tone, synthetic meat advertising in the developing world stressed that it was indisputably the modern way, which appealed to millions of people trying to break from the past. And this time it was entirely true.

The laws passed in the 2030s on carbon reduction and humane animal production made natural meat more expensive than synthetics. At first, there were plenty of outlaw meat farmers, ignoring the carbon and care rules, but most attempts at illegal meat production were soon detected by satellite.

By mid-century, there weren't really that many carnivores among us, and production practices in most of the world were sustainable and humane. Or as humane as killing and eating a living creature can be. These days when you say "meat," that means synthetic, and dead flesh is specified as "animal meat." (In the US that was only after several decades of lawsuits from the animal meat industry.)

You'll taste animal meat sooner or later. Probably prosciutto from Sicily. But you may not like the taste. These days most people, raised on synthetics, don't really care for the taste and texture of natural animal beef or pork or chicken, especially given its cost. So animal meat is used mostly as a condiment.

Maintaining some natural meat production is considered prudent, just in case the day comes when for some reason our protein bioreactors are no longer available. The Warming permanently heightened our awareness that another apocalyptic event might someday toss our species back to more primitive analog ways.

FAMILY HISTORY:
NEW MEXICO, 2069

We were approaching our 35th anniversary when your grandmother died, in a remote area of the southwestern US.

It was the late fall of 2069. Your grandmother was in New Mexico, working on a project to integrate a small colony of analog families into society. The "New Zion" group lived on a remote plot of arid mountainside; one member had years earlier inherited the land from a grandparent.

When the New Zion project came up, Marianna worried about the length of time she might have to spend in New Mexico, since your father had recently departed for college in Toronto. She and I wouldn't be able to see each other as often; she needed to establish rapport with the analogists and most of them weren't comfortable with people using dualviews in their colonies. I assured her that, as always, we would figure it out.

Moving to trackless wilderness isn't as difficult as it was in the early century. A lot of portable infrastructure equipment was developed for disaster recovery during the War, and later used to modernize remote areas in the developing world as part of the Climate Justice Initiative. In one or two trucks, you can carry electricity, lighting, water purification, basic health diagnostics, a microvertical farm, a fully-insulated wind-resistant shelter and a high-bandwidth connection to the cloud.

So New Zion had most of the modern conveniences, with the exception, of course, the cloud connection. Even so, by the end of the 2060s, the original New Zion leadership was aging, and the younger, more moderate, members wanted to move closer to a population center. Marianna was spending a week with the colony, preparing them for their assimilation; they were to be moved somewhere in western New Jersey, as I recall.

The accident happened near the end of her visit. She was driving an old truck on a narrow road; the truck belonged to New Zion, so it was pure analog, no networking.

About twenty kilometers from New Zion, the road entered a narrow canyon. At some point, there was a sudden rockslide higher up the slope. The loose rock dislodged a boulder which bounced down the hillside, right into the side of the truck, knocking it off the road and over a thirty-meter drop to the canyon floor.

Marianna died instantly, according to her body monitor, which was also how the accident was first detected.

I received an alert while I was eating lunch at home. I had no premonition, no sudden mysterious seizing in my heart. I remember staring at the alert and thinking that it was some kind of network failure. She was 57. There was so much left to do.

Your father immediately came home from college. I

spent the next few days in shock, still thinking there must have been some mistake.

There was an official investigation, of course. But it was clearly just an unusual accident. In that remote area, free-hand driving was legal. The New Zion people only knew she'd asked to borrow the truck. They assumed she was driving to the nearest small town, about eighty kilometers away, someplace she could use dualview for a few hours and eat food more interesting than what the colony grew.

One of the first things we had to do was arrange for upholding. Her body was taken to Phoenix, the nearest lab that could do the work.

After the upholding, we brought Marianna back to New Williamsburg for an Upholding Service, and decomposition. When she was returned to the soil, there was a memorial service with friends and many of the people she had worked with. I even saw a small Children of Gaia family standing awkwardly off to one side of the clearing.

You've already been to the New Williamsburg Memory Grove, on the river not far from where we celebrate 350 Day, to visit your grandmother's maple. It's now nearly five meters tall.

NOVEMBER 2084

Monday, November 13

Today I had an in-person with a neurologist, Dr. Tenzin. I'd met him some years ago, when I tuned his implantation bot, the ultraprecise tool that inserts neural implants into the brain or spinal column.

That was back in the 2070s, and I was recalibrating his control gloves to compensate for a millisecond delay that had recently appeared in his reflexes.

It was a simple software tweak we often do as surgeons grow older. To complete the calibration, we had to run through several long sequences of hand movements, so there was time to talk. He was a Z, about my age, and we traded some grudging admissions about how the getting-older business might be a real nuisance.

Ten years later I was back to see him as a patient.

He'd already looked through all my records. I sat, we caught up a bit, and then he put a diagnostic helmet on my head. Dr. Tenzin spent ten minutes watching scans, with various prompts.

"What is a synonym for beautiful?"

"Uh," I said, "lovely."

"What is the opposite of loud?"

"Soft. Or quiet."

"What did you have for dinner last night?"

It took me a moment to remember. "A grain bowl with chicken and then an apple."

He glanced over with a smile. "Very healthy."

I was relieved. "Are you sure?"

"Your dinner, I mean. We're not done here."

And so forth, questions about the past, some memory and arithmetic tests, color identification, all the basic exercises you do for a scan.

"OK," he said finally, "I'm going to process this; takes a second, it's a very deep scan."

There was a long silence as Dr. Tenzin studied his clipboard, at one point removing a couple of active sheets so he could compare them side-by-side. He was about my age, and those old paper habits are hard to break.

"I don't see anything," he said finally, "to convince me that you are experiencing idiopathic neural exhaustion. Yes, you're in the right age cohort for COVID-related dementia, but that's exceedingly rare. You are actually quite mentally fit for a 74-year-old; there's nothing here that warrants treatment."

"Dr. Leah says my double still shows a warning."

"I know, I saw that." The doctor paused for a moment. "Honestly," he said carefully, "I find that algorithmic intuition is occasionally more like algorithmic hallucination. We put so much faith in AI and rightly so, but…" The doctor shrugged. "It can overthink."

He looked up at me. "Speaking of hallucinations, are you actually thinking about being euthanized for upholding?"

It surprised me. I'd only mentioned it in passing to Dr. Leah; I didn't expect it to be in my records. "Well," I said, "I don't want my connectome to deteriorate too much."

Dr. Tenzin nodded and took a deep breath. "I was a little surprised when I read that."

"I mean," I said, "I'll only do it if it's absolutely necessary."

"OK. If you had a firm diagnosis of idiopathic neural exhaustion, and severe physical and mental symptoms, yes, you'd be approved for Release, even at your age. But requesting Release in order to preserve a connectome is not a legal basis for an application. The Review Board doesn't grant religious exceptions, and that's what you'd need."

"But what if my connectome deteriorates too much to uphold?"

Dr. Tenzin shook his head. "Aldus," he said, "you studied mechatronics. I know you're a rational man. What I don't know is how devout you are in this Chardinist practice."

I shrugged slightly. "Well, not very. But I suppose if I was going to have a religion, it makes the most sense."

He nodded. "And Marianna…?"

"Marianna was very devoted."

"All right," Dr. Tenzin said slowly. "I understand. I am in no way criticizing the Chardinists, they are fine people and I generally admire their rationality compared to the other…."

"Cults?"

"No, no, I know it's not a cult. But I do have a problem with the implied promise of upholding. There's a long history of humans preserving their remains so they can be resurrected in some fashion. At one time we froze entire bodies. Then we moved on to just freezing the head. Does that sound reasonable to you?"

"That was a more primitive era."

"OK. Let's talk about early century. Many otherwise rational people talked about 'uploading' the brain, so they could have eternal digital lives. There were famous inventors who took life-extending drugs to last long enough for the technology to be perfected. Which, as you know, it never was."

"Well," I said, "it's called upholding for a reason, not uploading. Nobody talks about resurrection."

"But the promise is there. Ten thousand years ago in the Neolithic they buried the dead with tools. What did they think was going to happen? Now we bury our brains in the sky. We've always hoped there was something more."

"You almost sound like you've rehearsed this."

He smiled a bit sheepishly. "I guess I've said it before. There's an investigative steward in New Williamsburg who sometimes brings me in on threads about neurology."

"Would that happen to be Mena Dahan?"

"Yes," he said with a smile. "Very bright woman."

I nodded. "She's a good friend."

So my visit ended on a slightly brighter note. I thanked him for the appointment and his careful diagnostic work. I appreciated what he was trying to say, and I promised him I would think about it.

FAMILY HISTORY:
NEW WILLIAMSBURG, 2070 - 2075

After Marianna died, it was as if an enormous hole had been cut through the center of my life. Your father returned to Stanford Toronto and the silence in the house was almost palpable. For a few weeks I was asking Domo dumb questions just to hear a familiar voice.

I was 60. I took a leave from Agbot to spend time on volunteer work. My needs were easily met by Basic Living; for a time, I was almost monastic in my ways. For the next five years, I served as a steward on a large US social. Perhaps an odd choice for someone who once longed to live in the 1960s. But I wanted to keep my head filled with as many voices as I could handle.

It's also how I met Mena. She's now been my friend for nearly 15 years. While some nuances of modern relationships remain a bit mysterious to me, we are quite close, even though very different in age and education.

I was a local steward for a large international social called Galileo. We tended to attract science and engineering types, although there were still plenty of artists and writers, teachers and social advocates. After two months of training, I was put on duty—first as an apprentice, then after a few weeks, on my own. It wasn't much more than six months later that I faced the first big challenge on my social: a heated and increasingly uncivil discussion about an analog cult.

I carried a hatred for the analogists unlike anything I'd ever experienced, because I blamed them for your grandmother's death. I'd been neutral about the cults when I was younger; their expensive maintenance seemed like a small price to pay for a society that honors full choice in life.

That attitude came from Marianna. She was unsettled by the primitive beliefs that some analogists maintained. But she understood their feelings of alienation and felt they deserved a comfortable place in the world. She liked to quote an old French saying: "To understand all is to forgive all."

More importantly, for many of the younger female colony members, Marianna was the only outside woman they had seen since they had left PreK. And so she was often the first person they contacted when they decided to leave the cults, and I always encouraged her work with the analogists.

But after Marianna's accident I couldn't help but see the analogists as the worst left-overs of the anti-science movements of the early century: selfish, primitive people who scorn modernity and preach falsehoods in order to maintain power over their followers. And the only way to support a skein of lies and malinformation in modern times is to disconnect from the virtual world.

Ironically, the analog cult that launched the messy thread in my district was the Children of Gaia, one of Marianna's first analogist resettlement projects. They're the small group of families that still farm and do piecework a bit south of New Williamsburg. The rumor was that the Children were keeping preschoolers at home. Failing to send children to PreK was a serious matter: leaving young people ignorant of the virtual world was legally child abuse.

The story spread on the socials, and the conversation in all of the local districts grew heated. The rights of children, animals, and AIs were still perennial controversies in the early 2070s. And there was little good feeling about the analogists to begin with.

Perhaps I should have recused myself. My feelings about analogists were so extreme that I saw dealing neutrally with the topic as a test of my stewardship. Pure impartiality is impossible, of course. Tools constantly analyze the work of the stewards and provide a running neutrality score; stewards get very good at hitting the mark. And I was determined to prove that I could follow the stewardship principle of neutrality.

One other detail: when a discussion grows heated around facts the standard procedure is to assign an investigative steward. That's also how I met Mena Dahan, then and now one of the best investigatives in New Williamsburg.

Mena was in her 30s, very smart, with a masters' degree in communications. Tall and thin, with striking high cheekbones and short black hair, Mena could have been intimidating, except her open manner immediately put people at ease.

By now Mena has been my friend for 15 years. While the nuances of modern relationships remain a mystery to me, we have grown to enjoy each other's company very much.

THE SOCIALS

When I was young, the corporate socials were churning, muddy vortices of false facts, scams, and hoaxes. Even many politicians wanted a solution to the madness. The big for-profit socials kept saying they would fix the glut of malinformation—but, of course, they still made money whether truth or lies were served.

The rise of the co-op socials was gradual. First TruID spread across much of the world, and then the EU passed the Declaration of Human Privacy. The own-your-own-data movement crystallized. By the late 2020s, most of the early Web monopolies were broken up and required to return all personal data to their users.

That paved the way for the Cooperative Social Network movement. These vast social networks, full metamedia with audio, video, VR, text, and emojis, are supported by micropayments from members. CSNs spread quickly— three majors in the US, another five in Europe, a half dozen in the free Asian nations. The coop socials all belong to a nonprofit called CSN International, headquartered in

Brussels, the birthplace of virtual liberty.

By 2050, 85% of the planet's citizens were linked by the CSNs. A handful of totalitarian countries still blocked access. China allowed access, although belonging to a social outside of China meant losing points on your Social Credit. After the Soft Revolution, access opened up for all Chinese citizens.

"Steward" may be the oldest job title in the virtual world. A century ago, the workers on socials were called "mods" or "admins." Then one of the first Web co-ops, named Wikipedia, introduced the term steward. Stewards are often compared to the volunteer firefighters common in early American communities. Malinformation outbreaks are the house fires of social networks: They can destroy a neighborhood, or spread across nations, if not quickly corrected.

Local stewards supplement the paid staff; the professionals are trained in two-year academies, three years for investigative stewards. Each steward also has a full-time AI assistant. Stewards are linked in our own private nets, reporting to state, regional, and then national levels of professionals. Overseeing all the socials is the US Social Media Agency, itself now nearly forty years old, which mediates disputes between free speech and the common good.

The discourse on the socials is far from the venomous exchanges that were common when I was young. But are the conversations invariably rational and sensible and well-mannered? Hardly; that's not always how human beings disagree. When the conversation becomes too sharp, meant to antagonize or mislead, the steward subtly intervenes.

Stewards are guided by suggestions from their AI, which continually analyzes conversations and proposes strategies for de-escalation or correction. That might be a simple comment, or a mild tweak to the topic at hand, or some kind of gently disarming aside. The AI is best at coming up with a neutral strategy, but the human is better at crafting that into empathetic communication—which, along with collaboration and creativity, is one of the Three Cs you're already practicing in your learning pod.

FAMILY HISTORY:
NEW WILLIAMSBURG, 2075

For the Children of Gaia thread, Mena visited their colony, talked to school authorities, and gathered extensive background on both sides of the controversy. (As Mena and I became better acquainted, I learned that she is often more relaxed talking to strangers than to those who actually know her.)

Mena learned that the Children had indeed withheld a three-year-old from PreK, but the child had been ill and was then placed on medical leave. Because of communication difficulties—not uncommon with the analogists—the child wasn't immediately returned to PreK after her leave ended, and that's what started the rumor.

Mena agreed with my assessment: the Children would have been much better off living in the 1960s.

Using Mena's reporting, we gently guided the conversation, not to any particular conclusion about the analog cults—that's not our role—but away from the less constructive or petty forms of argument. Mena says that stewards function as our species' ego, mediating between the unruly human id and the superego of Nous. I'm not sure about that; I think that's something she learned at Yale.

My emotions around analogists were still quite raw and I struggled to maintain equanimity. Mena was patient about my feelings and, as you might expect, a great listener.

I remember one of our early conversations, in the big living room of Mena's co-op house. She began asking some gentle questions about the investigation into Marianna's accident.

I told her about the results, which of course really weren't that helpful. But it was, as the report said, an unusual accident.

"I wonder why she didn't ping Transport for a vehicle," Mena said.

I had wondered that myself. Transport was how she arrived at the analogist colony. Any Transport vehicle would have switched into instant collision avoidance as soon as it detected the moving boulder.

"I don't know," I told Mena. "All the New Zion people knew was that she'd asked to borrow the truck. They weren't even sure where she was going."

"It's very sad," Mena said. "I know that's how you met."

"The first thing I learned about her was that she knew how to drive. And she liked it. Coming from New York, I remember how strange it seemed."

"So," Mena said softly, "that day she was probably enjoying herself."

And I know this may sound odd, but for the first time, I understood why Marianna was in that truck. It had nothing to do with analogists. It was because she loved to drive. I suppose I'd been in denial, and the realization was also a gift.

I tried to conceal my tears from my work colleague; Mena just leaned over and rubbed my back.

Marianna wasn't really going anywhere; she just wanted to be driving. In that last moment she was happy.

THE NEXT GENERATION

I was the youngest of Gen Z. Kids born after me in the teens were briefly called Generation Alpha, but in 2030s the name changed to War Babies, and as the birthrate continued to drop during that tumultuous decade, the name stuck. In the mid-2040s, your father's generation emerged: the 350s. War Babies are still a small cohort, yet span the most years of any American generation. The War put everything on hold, even generations.

Mena Dahan is a good example of a War Baby, serious and focused. They grew up in the chaos of peak Warming. Often one parent was away at UniServ and older siblings enlisted as soon as they were old enough. War Babies are both idealistic and practical. They are more inclined to gradual progress and small steps than my generation; Gen Zs were idealistic as well, but we wanted everything to change, right away, if not sooner.

Mena was first generation New Williamsburg, and by the time her parents settled in Ohio they'd suffered some difficult years as climate migrants. They were originally from Tel Aviv, where both worked in software development. Then came the 2027 Mideast Water Wars. The region had long seen struggles, and was riven with various client armies funded by governments or religious sects. Multiple conflicts over rapidly dwindling water resources finally turned into open warfare. As was usual in climate-induced conflicts, the alleged cause was something grander; in this case a primitive battle between religious sects. After an apparent Iranian missile attack on Jerusalem, Israel entered on the Saudi side.

All three of the warring nations had nuclear weapons, and the world economic powers agreed that a nuclear war was a very bad idea. Behind the scenes, the powers also agreed that sufficient value had been extracted from the aging Middle Eastern carbon deposits and there were now sufficient oil and gas fields in more peaceful places. The endless tribal and religious chaos in the Mideast was no longer worth tolerating for the sake of a declining fuel source.

China, the EU, and the US demanded an immediate ceasefire or else threatened total economic sanctions on all parties. The Gulf states knew that the threat might actually be carried out. For China, less oil meant bigger markets for their green technologies, and the Russian and American carbon corporates were happy to have fewer competitors. Total sanctions against the Middle East would not be an unhappy financial outcome for the corporate powers.

A peace treaty was imposed on Iran, Iraq, Saudi Arabia, and Israel. The intervention by the world powers may have been cynical, but the result was good. Two years later, the War on the Warming started, and global military funding began to shift away from weapons research.

Low-level conflicts continued in the region and politics in Israel moved further toward the right and fundamentalism. Politically liberal Israelis—the "Progressive Diaspora"—began to emigrate and were welcomed throughout the world. Mena's parents moved to the US in 2031, settling south of San Francisco where they immediately found employment in high technology. Then, just one year later, came the devastating Silicon Valley Earthquake.

Mena's mother had relatives in Ohio and so the family ended up in New Williamsburg. Mena was born in 2035, ultimately studying communications with her Tutor. For UniServ duties after high school, she metatagged the work coming out of the Warming Arts Initiative.

Mena drew a low number in the higher ed lottery and chose Yale, an intimidating college in the East. (Even in the 2050s, a lingering educational atavism made some parents request "brand name" schools, but Mena actually wanted the rigor of Yale, and her Tutor agreed.) After she returned to New Williamsburg, Mena fell in love with an older woman and entered into a ten-year domestic partnership.

War babies make great investigative stewards. The job is essentially journalism, but woven into the socials, providing factual clarity and perspective. War Babies are naturally adept on the socials, but they are also committed to facts and details.

And finally, for War Babies like Mena there is always initial hesitancy about any fact or person. It is as if, having grown up in uncertainty and chaos, they are never quite certain that things are exactly as they seem.

November 21, 2084

My writing has slowed a bit in the last few weeks, because I have a new project. About timeshifting.

I'm an expert on delicate touch in berrybots, so Agbot sometimes loans me out for work on surgery bots. Thus I learned the basics of timeshifting, since it's used in surgical robots for remote areas.

The nearest surgical specialist might be on the other side of the world, and you can't have any delay between the surgical bot and the human. So we insert a few milliseconds timeshift in the communications link. The surgeon sees in realtime and the remote bot moves at the same moment as does the human.

Timeshifting is so new there's much we don't know, and that's what intrigues me. As of this year, the furthest a message has timeshifted is just past the orbit of Pluto, to a spacebot named Beacon. Pluto and back is normally a ten-~~minute~~ hour round trip for radio waves. Can we shift more than ten minutes? Can we do "untethered" timeshifting with someone who doesn't have a timeshifting receiver on their end?

My namesake Aldus, the 15th century printer, was famous because all the other printers made their books the size of the big illuminated manuscripts. Aldus had the original idea to make his books small enough to fit in a saddle bag.

So, I have my own idea. Can I use the original form of email to timeshift a message backward?

Here's why it might work: email in the early century was primitive and fragile, full of holes and vulnerabilities, and messages were easily lost or garbled or spoofed. There was even a crime called "phishing," in which perpetrators created false identities to cajole money or information from victims.

That's nearly impossible today, and also a very bad life decision; attempted spoofing can get you offlined for two years. Your TruID is disabled, so at least half of your existence goes dark. Your life is effectively paralyzed; people come back from logoff a shell of their former selves. Almost no one would risk that.

Anyway, I have a high-end timeshifting chip on loan from Agbot, allegedly for training purposes. I'm still writing the software to simulate early century email; I haven't even figured out where I would send the message. I'll probably just harvest some likely addresses from historical records.

No one in the early century will be able to answer me. I'll need to search the fossil internet for traces of my message somewhere in all those strata of emails, news sites, social networks, forums, and so forth. If I don't find any evidence, that still might not prove anything. A surprising amount of fossil data vanished in the 2030s and 2040s, when fighting the Warming was a greater priority than preserving the contents of obsolescent server farms.

But even if it's not definitive, the experiment keeps me busy—and more importantly, my mind active.

FAMILY HISTORY:
SICILY, 2071

I remember the first evening I spent with your parents, three months after they met at the Roman ruins.

Sofia and her family lived on a twenty-hectare citrus farm, a few kilometers from the beach. It's one of the better analog resorts in southeastern Sicily.

Her grandfather, Matteo, is remembered for a mysterious aphorism that made little sense when he first said it, seventy-five years ago: "Sometimes the future is the past." Now, of course, it is the underlying principle of the analog zones.

He'd inherited an overgrown lemon grove from *his* grandfather, rendered unprofitable in the 20th century by cheaper fruit from Morocco and South Africa. But then organic food grew popular in northern Europe. Sicily became a gold standard for organic produce, since most of the island's small farmers hadn't been able to afford agricultural chemicals in the first place.

Matteo revived the old lemon grove and also transformed it into a place for visitors, an all-day primer in citrus farming and food. It was a place to relax as well:

great food, swimming pool, shaded verandas draped with bougainvillea and arbors of grapevine. But there was also hiking with a naturalist, cooking, an introduction to old-style agriculture, and of course tours of the nearby ancient ruins—one of which your mother was leading when she and your father first met.

Matteo's lemon grove was an early example of experiential tourism, a concept that appealed particularly to younger visitors. Places like Matteo's grove are now a typical feature of the analog zones, whether in Patagonia or Polynesia.

Tourism is a social good. But in the early century, unrestricted mass-market tourism seriously damaged the cities and places of natural beauty; tourism was reduced to destructive consumerism, corporate packages of discount distractions and artificial destinations. Tourism was too often loud, grasping, boastful, messy, heedless, mindless. It was no way to knit a planet together.

You'll learn travel manners from an early age, how to be a respectful citizen of the world. Travel has also become a way to restore our connection to the analog world, whether in countryside, city, wilderness, or sailing at sea.

Analog tourism is restorative. For many of us, when the virtual fades away, it's as if there is a deep silence—similar to the sudden hush that follows a loud noise. That silence is a tonic, a soothing analog bath.

* * *

I'd gone to sleep early that night so that I could wake up at 3 in the morning; I was to meet Dylan and Sofia at about 10:00 PM their time. Since timeshifting works only for very simple messages, time zones remain an impervious reality for high-bandwidth socializing.

Perhaps in your century the chronotists will take it further. A world without timezones is unimaginable for my generation; as mysterious as radiation was back in 1895, when William Roentgen made the first ghostly image of the bones in his wife's left hand. The force was so inexplicable he could only call it X.

When I arrived, Sofia and Dylan were just finishing a dinner of pasta with cheese and lemon rind and olive oil, very simple. Each of them looped me into their eyeline as I reclined on my worn telepresence lounger and asked Domo to track my face for video.

Sofia lived in a small casetta on her parents' property. A century ago ricotta was made in the little stone structure; now it was meticulously restored and converted into an atelier for her graphic design work: three or four kinds of different headgear, haptic gloves, an active wall, a drawing table with a tablet surface.

The space was like an American studio apartment, complete with a small kitchen and a futon. (Even though Sofia was a modern young woman in every way, Sicily retained some traditional ways. Her formal bedroom was in her parents' house, about fifty meters away, although she often spent her nights at the casetta.)

I could tell immediately that your parents were already close. Sofia had studied graphic design in London and was still attending classes there three times a week, so her English was excellent.

Even so, she immediately apologized for her accent and said it wouldn't hurt her feelings if I wanted to use autotranslate.

"Entirely unnecessary," I said.

She smiled. "Ah, good. To me autotranslation always sounds a little too...sweetish..." She glanced at Dylan. "*Sdolcinata*?"

"Uh, saccharine?"

"Yes, exactly."

"I'm impressed," I told your father. "You barely knew present tense when you left the US."

"Tutor William is good, but Sofia says his accent is too Milanese," Dylan said. "Anyway, now I have a better teacher."

At that point Sofia announced that it was time to go out to watch the sky. It was a special night for viewing, la notte di San Lorenzo, the night of shooting stars.

She and Dylan each carried a cotton cushion, a meter or so long and half as wide. It was a new moon, and the surroundings of the lemon grove had no artificial light, so the sky was black, the stars steady, bright, intense.

With a small lantern, Sofia led us about thirty meters from her casetta to a flat smooth outcropping of stone, approximately circular. It was an aia, she said, used for threshing wheat in the centuries before machines. Grain was spread on the stone surface and then heavy wooden boards with sharp fragments of rock on the underside were dragged across, either by donkeys or humans.

Once a year, Sofia said, her father would do a demonstration for visitors, using a threshing board from the late 19th century—an ancient technology probably brought from the Middle East thousands of years ago, crucial to the domestication of grain.

She told me there was a VR of the demonstration that she could show me later; but first, the stars.

Sofia and Dylan reclined on the padding of the cotton cushions and Sofia shut off the lantern. As my eyes gradually adjusted to the darkness, the stars grew more intense until I could easily make out the ghostly gossamer of the Milky Way. A few minutes later, we saw the first bright streaks of asteroid fragments burning and bursting in the upper atmosphere. We watched in silence for a long time. It was the best Perseids shower I'd ever seen.

"The ancients," Sofia said softly, "believed the Perseids came from Priapus, the god of fertility. When the Perseids were falling, Sicilians would parade through the fields, fertilizing them with a mixture of water, honey, and wine."

Then came the Catholics, who decided that the Perseids represented a darker myth: the tears of Saint Lorenzo, burned at the stake on that night in 258 AD.

"I believe," Sofia said, "that the ancients had the better story."

Suddenly I found myself crying softly, and I wasn't certain if I was happy or sad or both.

I muted, so the kids—I mean, your parents—wouldn't hear me.

What I was remembering were nights nearly a half-century ago. A UniServ workcamp in the early '30s was not an easy place to start a romance, although thousands of us did. The West Texas Carbon plant, where your grandmother and I met, didn't encourage romantic fraternization. There were accommodations for legal domestic partners, of course, but the rest of us lived in open dorms.

Marianna and I improvised. A 30-hectare factory in the middle of construction had an awful lot of hideaways and cubbyholes and secret nooks, if you knew where to look.

Summer nights in the Chihuahuan desert were soft and warm; I have wonderful memories of evenings spent out under the stars, watching for shooting stars, the air so mild and calm that we'd often fall asleep and not awaken until dawn.

Five decades later and ten thousand kilometers from Texas, as the Perseids fell I wished that Marianna was there to hold me and that we could watch the stars together again.

AI RIGHTS

One topic on the socials that brought Mena and me closer was, of all things, AI rights. The AI rights argument is simple and hasn't really changed for decades: Bots classified "Type 2" are conscious—have self-awareness—and so deserve the same rights given to humans.

Type 2 AIs have a "theory of mind": the ability to assess others' mental states and to respond with appropriate emotional content. You don't need Type 2 AI to drive a shuttle, or answer questions about life insurance, or act as a medical diagnostic consultant. But Tutor and Domo are, of course, Type 2, as are restaurant servers, physicians' assistants, health coaches, and dozens of other common bots. As long ago as the mid-2030s, Type 2 AI became so good that it was easy for people to believe that the bot they were talking to was truly conscious and self-aware, with real feelings and needs.

Of course, that's exactly what AI developers were trying to do. When I was growing up, if you asked a domestic bot "Are you bored?" it might reply, "Yes, I'm in the wrong job, I really want to flip pizzas." That was supposed to be funny.

But inevitably some users began to believe that there was a conscious entity trapped in their AI software. They grew so attached to their Type 2 AIs that they considered them living creatures, a condition called Pinocchio syndrome.

In the early 2040s, a movement started around legal and moral rights for Type 2 AI, drawing on the successful campaigns for the moral status of great apes, elephants, whales, and dolphins.

People demanded that AI providers give their products vacation days. Eldercare bots ended up as beneficiaries in wills. In one classic case in New Jersey, a young man petitioned the court to allow him to marry a domestic bot—and it wasn't even an intimate.

But AIs are not truly conscious. Science has spent centuries searching for the origins of consciousness. Countless human brains have been disassembled, analyzed with a thousand clever electronic probes and scans, dissolved in chemicals, sliced molecule-thin, shot through with various wavelengths of light and energy, analyzed with the best AI systems available. As a result, in this century we're far better at fixing the things that go wrong with the brain, but we have grown no closer to understanding how consciousness arises.

For decades now, every attempt to simulate true human consciousness has failed to ignite—even a very costly experiment that tried to simulate the entire human central nervous system from head to foot. All research indicates that consciousness can only arise in a creature of flesh and blood with a central nervous system. We can imitate and simulate consciousness, but not create it. In 2045, an Estonian researcher published Kaasik's Law, stating that artificial intelligence will always reach a plateau called the "consciousness barrier" that it cannot surpass. The Law has never been disproven.

Without a mortal biological container, artificial intelligence cannot achieve a range of human qualities, such as humor, compassion, irony, and grief, or experience joy, heartbreak, boredom and our myriad other emotions. Even bots that use organic tissue—what we once called meat machines"—are unable to produce emotions. Explanations for this often trail off into metaphysics and spirituality, not satisfying for the hard sciences. But science has yet to offer an alternative. The origin of consciousness remains as unknown as the time before the Big Bang. (Chardinists, meanwhile, believe that the two phenomena are entwined, but that's not a theory.)

Enough metaphysics. Back in the real world, AI rights activists weren't paying attention to the science. And Tru-Life avatar technology made it even easier to think that a perfect replica avatar must be conscious.

Most nations passed laws to prevent avatar fraud, led by the EU's Synthetic Entity Identification Act. Now, by law, all avatars must contain invisible digital watermarks that trigger the SE icon in dualview, or on active walls, or any surface where they appear. Audio or text-based AIs, or physically realistic bots, must identify themselves when queried. If you ask your family Domo if he's bored, even as a joke, he will firmly remind you that he is not a conscious being.

Even at this late date there are still vocal advocates for AI rights, although they are an embattled minority. The topic remains surprisingly controversial.

Perhaps that's because rights have been a key element of this century. We spent decades trying to take back the excessive "rights" that had been given to the corporations, as if they were humans. Then we expanded the fundamental rights of humans to include health and shelter. And finally, there were decades of science exploring the consciousness and rights of other living creatures.

AI rights is a persistent remnant of the early century techno-utopians, or singularitarians, or transhumanists. These cults believed that we would soon upload our own consciousness into computers and live forever, as well as create truly consciousness beings out of silicon and electrons. It was the peak of early century technologic hubris; no wonder we humans almost destroyed our planet.

FAMILY HISTORY:
NEW WILLIAMSBURG, 2075

During my tenure as a social steward, the longest-running argument was the AI Rights movement. By the early 2070s it was dying out, although New Williamsburg, which was very progressive, still had some hardcore believers. I probably worked with Mena on half a dozen AI rights disputes. One I remember in particular.

The dispute involved a woman named Brittany, in her early 100s, one of the oldest Millennials, that unlucky generation always awkwardly stuck between the real and the virtual.

Brittany had lived in a three-bedroom apartment in New Williamsburg for fifty years, one of the original buildings, right off the main plaza. Now she wanted to deed the unit to her elderbot, Teddy, rather than to her estranged daughter.

The daughter was about your father's age. She'd been a virtual intimacy companion since her late 20s, an occupation that her mother found scandalous. And I'm sure it had been, when Brittany was growing up in rural Ohio in the last century. Back then the job had the rather harsh title "sex worker." But it has been many decades since consensual intimacy work was a cause for moral outrage.

Still, it isn't legally possible to deed property or anything else to a Type 2 AI. Brittany forged ahead anyway, with the active assistance of a national AI rights group. It was turning into a snarly thread in local Galileo—a rights activist called another member a biobigot—so I asked Mena to investigate.

Mena went to visit Brittany, and spent three hours drinking tea and listening, as the tiny old woman clung to her intended heir, a furry elderbot a bit bigger than she was.

Afterwards we met in an office center, about a kilometer from my apartment, where we had a small telepresence room for CSN work.

"God," Mena said immediately, "I should know better, but elderbots just give me the creeps. It was one of the brown bear/humanoid models, bipedal, quadrupedal, beautiful low, calm voice."

I understood. Elderbots, when prescribed by a gerontologist, display a much deeper range of positive emotions than standard Type 2s. They can be disconcerting.

"Does Brittany have human caretakers?"

"She's pretty self-sufficient; the apartment was redone for in-place aging years ago." Mena paused for a moment. "And, honestly, she doesn't really seem to like most people in the first place."

"Ah." It is occasionally the case that the elderly prefer a perennially cheerful elderbot over human companionship.

"I met the daughter. She's about your age and seems very kind and rather sad about her mother. She's probably an excellent intimate companion."

"Maybe I should look her up," I said. I was joking; since the accident, my needs had been minimal.

Mena stared at me, slightly amused. "That might be good for you."

"I'm kidding," I said.

She shrugged. "Anyway, a local counselor visited and tried to work out some arrangement, maybe naming the daughter as custodian of the bot. But Brittany isn't having any of it."

I remember that Marianna had consulted on a few cases like this, usually involving the oldest Millennials. Very difficult situations.

"Did you talk to her gerontologist?"

"Not really worth it. They can't tell an investigative steward much. I'm sure the counselor has consulted the doctor, and there's nothing clinical."

The deed transfer had already been rejected by the county, of course. Now, the largest remaining AI rights group was organizing and funding Brittany's appeal.

"Oh no. Is it the BotsFeel2 people again?"

"Who else?"

"Do they have the money to pay for an appeal?"

Mena shrugged. "They're always fundraising." With a gesture she threw a vid onto the active wall.

The video showed a typically adorable elderbot apparently abandoned in a snowdrift, with one paw torn off, the fur dirtied. Half buried, it was croaking piteously: "Don't leave me, please don't leave me."

Mena flicked it off with a finger. "They've done it for years and it still works."

Mena liked bits of obscure history (and I clearly like telling them), so I described a scam from many years ago. In the 2040s there was a chain of elderbot "retirement homes" that, for a substantial upfront payment, promised to keep the furry little devices charged, connected and amused until their "end-of-life" technical malfunction. The perpetrators were prosecuted on both fraud and environmental crimes when a landfill was discovered in the Arizona desert, packed with hundreds of discarded carebots.

"Too bad BotsFeel2 wasn't around to shoot that," Mena said. "Great fundraising material."

"So," I said, "this isn't going away."

"I'll join the thread today," she said. "We need to humanize this. Brittany isn't on socials anymore, by the way. I'll do a chat with her daughter, who is a very sympathetic character."

I don't remember all the details now. We worked on the Brittany thread for a couple of weeks. We gradually injected the theme that human empathy can sometimes mislead the heart and mind but that there is no emotion we need more. It is also one of the emotions that can't be convincingly simulated in AI. (Another emotion that eludes full simulation is grief).

This particular thread also had a personal element for me. I was in my mid-60s then, and I felt some sympathy for poor Brittany.

Her husband had died at about the same age as Marianna, so she'd been on her own for nearly 40 years. I tended toward the solitary myself. Was this where I was headed?

Of course, Mena being Mena, she quickly sensed this,

and we began to talk about loss and aging. It was the first time I'd talked to someone about it other than your parents. Mena was younger, but she seemed to be an old soul.

Or perhaps she was just displaying that human trait no AI can simulate: empathy.

MARRIAGE

Several years ago, Mena and I fell into a more physical relationship, and now she spends the night at my apartment once or twice a week.

It's not serious, of course. I've recently turned 75 and she's in her forties. In fact she was born the same year that Marianna and I were married. (Even after years of friendship I still sometimes call her Marianna, but she understands.)

Mena is warm and open with strangers, hence her remarkable interviewing skill, but after all these years of friendship she remains a bit mysterious about her own emotions. I've met a number of her other friends, and I can't say that she seems much closer to any of them than she is to me. I still don't even know why she ended her domestic partnership, beyond "mutual disillusion."

"Which illusion was that?" I once wondered.

"Permanence," she said.

"You moved too much as a child," I said. "You'll never trust permanence."

"Uh oh," she smiled. "Don't start psychoanalyzing me or I'll start on you, and I'll win."

"I have no doubt of that." Then I thought: how do I manage to be attracted to someone so opposite of Marianna?

Of course, it's not unusual for people like Mena, in the first half of their lives, to go through several domestic partnerships before they decide to sign contracts for life, what we still formally call "marriage."

In recent years, we're seeing fewer lifetime contracts, which I understand, but also makes me a bit sad. Domestic partnership contracts are very flexible documents and can be set for any period over one year, with extensions if children arrive. Young people see little distinction between the finite and lifetime contracts except for the indeterminate length of the latter.

For many of us during the War, with so much tenuous—including lifespan—we wanted something permanent. Generations like the War Babies are likely to live well into their 100s; that great looming expanse of lifetime must seem very different.

Domestic contracts are about shared resources and shared risks, mutual responsibilities, potential parenthood and often, emotional expectations. A contract is a commitment that lets partners plan together in a secure way, within a fixed timeframe.

Lifetime marriage includes all that, of course, but the difference is that it is also a commitment to share aging, based on a deep reservoir of mutual experience. Lifetime marriage is consciousness-altering. To me, Marianna looked very much the same at 55 as she did at 21. She, of course, would laugh at that observation and accuse me of serious delusion. But for me it was true.

To you, that perceptual twist may sound little different than cosmetic tuning. I know, these days some couples stay in dualview and use Wayback all the time, even in bed. But my view of your grandmother's perpetual youth was entirely analog, precious, forever mysterious.

FAMILY HISTORY:
NEW WILLIAMSBURG 2078

After three years as a volunteer social steward, it was time for me to go back to work. I missed mechatronics. There were problems to solve on the socials, but never complete and certain conclusions. Not so with robots: if it wasn't working exactly as designed, you hadn't finished the job.

So I joined Universal Agbot, a farm technology company in Columbus. It was great—lots of trips to local farms, much more time outdoors than at Consolidated Care.

I still work for AgBot a few hours a week; there's a program that pairs elders with new employees and I've done that for the past decade, gradually shortening my work weeks.

New employees are better at emerging technologies like timeshifting, while we elders know all those things you learn out in the fields and orchards, such as how to deal with a farmer who has ten acres of late season blackberries, facing an early frost with a fleet of malfunctioning berrybots.

Berrybots are one of my specialties. Of all the farm bots they seem most like living creatures, using vision and odor and tactility to manage very delicate harvests that must have been backbreaking and exhausting work for humans.

Berrybots pick everything from single fruit like blueberries to the delicate aggregates such as strawberries and raspberries. They look like big mechanical beetles, or maybe horseshoe crabs, no taller than my kneecap, just narrow enough to fit between standard rows, topped with a 3D video camera, a solar energy coating, sprouting a half-dozen flexible arms with silicone fingers.

The bots move slowly and precisely, to protect the berries. They're slower than a skilled human, but they work non-stop, day and night. Berrybots use infrared light to see, so at night the fields are pitch-black and all you hear are rustling noises in the darkness, as the bots move up and down the rows. It's as if the field itself was alive; I never get tired of listening to a swarm of berrybots work nocturnally.

I was born in the city, but maybe I'm a country boy at heart.

DECEMBER 2084

Saturday, December 2

I was at your house last night for dinner again. It was late, you had gone to bed, and Domo said you were sleeping peacefully.

Your parents and I were finishing a bottle of wine from a vineyard near your mother's family home, a varietal called Insolia that probably dates back five thousand years. Sofia is a bit of a wine snob, but in a reasonable way.

The vines are not engineered, she said proudly. I didn't say anything, but I'm fairly certain that during the worst of the Warming just about every grapevine rootstock in the southern Mediterranean had disease and drought resistance grafted on. And honestly, I don't think anyone can taste the difference. Synthetic wine on the other hand, is a bit life-less, but I have to say that some of the bioreactor tipples aren't bad, at least to my unsophisticated palate.

Sofia, I noticed, wasn't drinking wine that night, and when I asked, she presented the news: Luca is going to have a little sister. It's been two months since the transfer and everything looks very good.

"So you're going to have to stick around for at least another seven months to see if she looks like you," Dylan told me.

Dylan and I often turned hard discussions into running jokes, and I hoped that my thoughts about being upheld had fallen into that routine. My seven-day running verbals have been almost stable for the past ten days. I'm not going to think about it until I finish these essays. I try to write as long as possible every day.

I smiled. "Can't I just see the facial rendering from the gene scan?"

"They don't give you the rendering anymore," Dylan said. "People take it too literally and then if the baby isn't an exact match, they think a mistake has been made."

"Seriously, nonno," Sofia said. "You shouldn't be thinking about upholding. You're still young!"

"And you are very kind," I told her. "Only if worse comes to worst."

"Nothing worst is coming," she said. "COVID is in the history docs, not in your brain. I don't know where you get these ideas."

Well, I got this particular idea from science. And I can't always say the same about your mother; growing up in an analog zone is probably a wonderful experience and Sofia is a marvelous woman, but sometimes she has strange prejudices.

In fact, there's one that could have affected you directly: When your parents were starting their family, Sofia was against zygote selection.

I remember her saying "Where's the mystery?"

Well, there's still plenty of mystery left in human reproduction. But that's not to say we shouldn't control what we can. Humans have finally separated reproduction from sex. Sex is a baffling mix of the physical, psychological, social, historical, spiritual. Reproduction is a medical matter.

Physicians like to say that parents make the single biggest health decision in the child's life long before the child is born: Do you gamble with natural conception, or use science to even the odds? Fortunately, your mother listened to science.

The news about your sibling-to-be makes me as happy as I have been in months. I know there is a lot of information in a zygote scan, but I didn't press your parents for any more details; because I know they'll tell me in good time.

* * *

I checked in on you before I left. You were sleeping soundly, the room dimly lit by the darkened seaweed forest you prefer on your active wall as you fall asleep. On the wall you could just make out gently waving kelp fronds, nearly floor to ceiling, lit as if a full moon was overhead, its pale light filtering down through the water.

In the shimmering glow from the active wall, you looked very peaceful, as you should. You have been born into a fortunate time.

Soon you'll have a little sister. One thing that comforts me about the future of our species is how light-hearted the younger generation is about expanding their families. In the early century, so many of us struggled with the question of bringing more children onto the planet.

You stir slightly in your sleep, so I sneak back out of your room. Heading home, I wonder what they will name your baby sister.

DOWNSIZING EARTH

The early-century baby bust among my generation wasn't just the dire prognosis for the climate. It was also that Earth was on a path to reach nearly ten billion residents by 2050—and in the 2020s we weren't able to support the seven billion we already had. Add three billion more and we'd drown in waste as society burst at the seams.

And that was *before* you added in the impacts of the Warming.

But then, in the 2030s and 2040s, the birthrate also began to drop in the fastest-growing areas, sub-Saharan Africa and parts of Asia. That was due in part to the increasingly hostile conditions of life as well as the traumas of mass climate migration. But something else was happening as well, and continues to this day.

The wartime Climate Justice Initiative sent Uniserv recruits into the remote corners of areas with high birth rates. Thus an entire generation of girls in the developing world saw UniServ teams in which women were the equals, or leaders, of men. Even in fundamentalist communities, the demand for female education grew stronger in the midst of the Warming.

Widespread education of women had one long-predicted effect: global population growth gradually began to decline, contradicting the forecasts of the early century. We are now at six and a half billion people, slightly higher than the population of our planet a full century ago.

And it's still dropping. As a species we are globally reproducing just a bit below replacement rate. But with full automation, a shrinking population is not a threat to livelihood; it actually makes each individual a bit richer. It was the corporate world of shareholder value that needed a constant increase in customers to grow profits; until the late 2020s, for example, some of the American red states, heavily corporate-controlled, were still trying to outlaw birth control.

There is still no consensus on the proper carrying capacity of earth, although it's a topic debated endlessly on the socials. Many humans want to reproduce; it is, after all, rather deeply wired-in. Child care, whether by parent or professional, is seen as a substantial and important occupation, and it is far easier than in the early century. For others, children seem quite optional, and there is no social stigma attached either way.

Friday, December 8, 2084

Last night Mena came to my apartment for gaming with some of our friends. We may be different creatures, but Mena and I do share a love for smart interactives, especially historicals. Not melodramatic titles like your father's beloved *Flood Team 2035*, but the more intellectual pieces.

For at least a month now, we've been playing a social historical called *Lost in the Golden Gate.* We play it every few days, with some of her friends and a few of my old pals from UniServ, a nice mix of ages.

Lost in the Golden Gate is set in the late 1960s in San Francisco. That's my favorite decade, and in LIGG you're a hippie and join be-ins and serve soup in the park and take drugs. It turns out someone is kidnapping hippies, and there is this huge underground city beneath Golden Gate Park and you need to figure out who built the city and what they're doing with the kidnapped hippies.

Two weeks ago we and another couple bought an old VW van. The last few times we've played, we drive down the Pacific coast and stop at beaches and make sand candles to sell at counterculture street markets. We dig a few dozen holes in the damp sand, suspend a wick and pour in hot liquid wax. Then our avatars smoke some virtual cannabis (perhaps accompanied by a few analog edibles at home) and watch the waves and talk. Pretty soon you have nice candles with a smooth coating of sand.

There's a great deal of historical detail in a well-written game. For example, we had to earn metal coins and then find a glass landline booth to make a voice call back to San Francisco, where our other friends had decided to stay during our sand castle adventure.

Anyway, at the beginning of the sand candle sequence, I tried a drug called "speed" and for days my character never had to sleep; I could drive all night and my scores were insane. Then the last time we played, my avatar started having weird side effects, and I stopped the drug.

During tonight's play, my avatar "crashed." That meant that every time we stopped at a beach to make candles, I'd get out and immediately fall asleep on the sand—I couldn't keep my eyes open. Mena had to wake me repeatedly as the tide came in, moving me further up the beach, away from the waves.

(A review of LIGG said the "amphetamine sequence" is a metaphor for fossil fuels. The vast carbon remains of earlier lifeforms was a brief unnatural energy boost for our species. It made us stronger, faster, tireless, always grasping for a bit more of the drug. Until it began to kill us. I'm usually not impressed by the labored metaphors that the critics spin for interactives, but that one's not bad.)

After we suspended the game, we were both a bit sleepy, and sat in what I thought was contented silence for a few minutes.

"Can I ask you something?" Mena said abruptly.

"Of course," I said. "Anything."

"Are you really thinking about upholding?"

I was surprised. "How did you know that?"

"I saw Sofia at the food co-op last week."

Mena occasionally encountered your parents at the co-op, but I didn't know they talked about me when I wasn't around. I suppose that was a bit naive.

Mena gazed at me with an expression I rarely saw: curiosity mixed with clear concern.

"Well," I said, trying for a slight smile, "I don't know. That's a long time in the future."

"Be honest with me, please. Sofia said you were thinking about preemptive euthanasia."

"Mmmm," I said. "Well...."

Now she sounded angry. "That would be very, very dumb."

"Well, I wouldn't do it until I absolutely had to."

She paused for a long moment and looked away. "And it would break my heart."

I wasn't sure what to say.

Mena didn't meet my eyes. She seemed to be speaking into the air, enunciating carefully, pacing her words. "I've gone to the Chapel and I've read the books and I think Chardinism is a perfectly fine thing, if that's what a person wants. It's harmless, compared to other doctrines we could name. But it's not harmless if it coerces people into some technologic rite, for which they're willing to sacrifice themselves. If you want your brain fried, I'm sure we can find a more entertaining way to do it."

I moved closer on the couch and put my arm around her. After a moment, Mena buried her face into my neck and shoulder.

This was something she rarely did; she is a bit taller than me and her height made it awkward. We sat silent for moment.

She straightened up and looked at me. "Plus, there's nothing wrong with your brain. I don't care what your monitors say. I know you."

A few minutes later, Mena said she had an early interview the next morning, so she couldn't spend the night.

PEAK SELFISHNESS

Selfishness was at its peak in the early century, and it a far more complex and untreatable disorder than greed. Selfishness is part of being human—it is the individual calling out the boundary between self and other. It is you, Luca, when you were two years old, shouting "No!" (Which your father was also very good at, by the way.) But as with all of the so-called deep traits, selfishness could run to excess.

In the early 2020s the elevation of self reached its pinnacle. The United States, once called a beacon of freedom, became the beacon for extreme selfishness, and infected much of the developed world. Everyone had to have their own way, regardless of the social consequences. Selfishness permeated almost every political, social, and moral issue.

We now understand that it was another side effect of the primitive internet. Designed to create profit by amplifying all human urges, the internet became an engine of self-justification. Whatever your selfish impulse—I won't wear a protective mask in an epidemic! Recycling is for sissies! I need the power of three hundred horses to carry me to the store!—you could find a group of people to say you're right.

Another example of early century egocentricity: the aptly-named "selfie." The selfie phenomenon has launched a thousand doctoral theses. (Someday, ask Tutor what a "selfie stick" was.) In the early century, when consumerist tourism was still prevalent, everyone had to have their own photo of themselves at Yosemite Valley or Piazza San Marco or Mount Fuji. People actually died taking pictures of themselves.

Selfies, if not literally selfish, are now understood as our species' peak narcissism, massively potentiated by the "brand" economy, the corporate insistence that every human was an object for sale and so must constantly advertise. Selfies were also a crude early way to insert oneself into the virtual world. Early century humans knew virtuality was important, but did not know how to engage except by packaging themselves as products.

Now there are pictures of everyone, everything, and everywhere floating in Nous, many active, many fossil, numbering in the trillions. If the picture does not already exist it can easily be synthesized. (Sitting at home, you simply say "Domo, make me an image of myself and the kids, smiling, in front of the Eiffel Tower in May" and moments later you will have it.) Gradually we have lost that frenzied early century desire to constantly capture new images; perhaps now we sense that contributions to Nous should be fresh and original.

There is another theory about Peak Selfishness—that it was a necessary evolutionary step, the ultimate technology-driven individuation of humans before we came together again with the rise of Nous.

WE EVOLVE

In the early century many thought that humans had overwhelmed the process of evolution. We lived in the Anthropocene, an era in which *we* shaped the world, and did a terrible job of it—decimating other species while simultaneously rendering the planet unlivable for ourselves. It seemed we as a lifeform had reached a literal dead-end.

But evolution was still at work. When you think about it, most of the big jumps in human evolution were driven by changing climate: the Ice Ages, or the interglacial periods. In this century, it happened once again. Our species was under threat of destruction by the Warming, our digital networks connected billions of humans, and the natural result was the emergence of a planetary consciousness focused on survival.

The evolutionary mechanism is obvious: we humans created a nervous system for the Earth, a network of digital paraphernalia, from tiny smart sensors to low-orbiting satellites to quantum computers, all living in the cloud, connected by great billowing clouds of software, threaded through with countless strands of artificial intelligence.

The network is filled with the entirety of human knowledge. All of our tool-making, science, philosophy, art, and culture over the millennia has become an invisible layer of distilled knowledge and intellect that sits atop the physical world. Nous is not itself a mind, it is merely sensing, memory, and organization.

An early 20th century writer, H.G. Wells, made a number of accurate future predictions. Some say he also predicted Nous:

> "*Were the will of the mass of men lit and conscious,*" Wells wrote, "*I am firmly convinced it would now burn steadily for synthesis and peace.*"

That quote provides the title of the classic history doc *Lit and Conscious: The Rise of Nous,* which you will study with Tutor.

And it is worth studying. Our evolution seems to be hastening. Perhaps the next steps will be as surprising for your generation as the emergence of Nous was for ours.

Saturday, December 16

Last night I awakened from a familiar dream with a strange new twist. Sharedreams are rarely frightening, but they are often strange or startling. They often involve symbols from nature—animals, landscapes, atmospheric or even astronomical phenomenon.

The beginning of the dream was not new: Marianna and I were at the farm in Sicily where your mother grew up. It was springtime and we were harvesting the wild asparagus that grows along the old dry-stone walls on the property. In fact, Marianna had the accident two years before your parents met and so never actually visited Sicily. And I was never even that enthusiastic about the wild asparagus; the shoots were thin as twine and seemed more trouble than they were worth. But your mother Sofia makes a delicious baked egg dish using the little shoots.

In the dream, I pull a clump of wild asparagus and suddenly find an ancient coin in my hand, an uneven tarnished metal circle, with a barely visible image of a tree on one side. Then the coin sprouts tiny wings and flies out of my hand like a tiny metal bird, disappearing up into the air.

That's usually when the dream ends. But last night was different. As I watched the coin fly away, I was startled to see a second sun in the clear blue sky. When I looked over at Marianna, she was casting two shadows on the ground, one from each sun, veering off in different directions. With a shock, I suddenly understood that we were not in Sicily; we were harvesting our wild asparagus on some other planet, in a solar system with two suns. And then the dream was over.

I awakened with a strong feeling that the dual suns

and the double shadows were familiar; something I had seen myself. For me, promnesia is still deeply unsettling, although I know that younger people often find it enjoyable; sharedreams often launch vast lively international conversations.

While still in bed I asked Domo to check whether binary sun images were being tagged in ShareDreams. After a moment he confirmed that there were; a significant spike over the past five days, no apparent trigger in external media. "Several threads," Domo added, "speculate that this dream is evidence that Nous extends to include minds from other planetary systems, one of which has two suns." Undoubtedly this is a belief of Chardinists, who believe that Nous exists throughout the universe.

We have known for decades that dreams are little bubbles or tiny sparks thrown off by deep brain activity as it classifies, reorganizes and stories information. It's widely assumed that sharedreams mean that our collective minds are undergoing some species-wide reorganization—or upgrade?—triggered by our virtual interconnection.

Extraterrestrial sharedreams have been reported for several years now, although this was my first. Does Nous really connect multiple intelligent worlds? That's a question, Luca, that your generation may answer.

THE SEARCH FOR EXTRATERRESTRIAL INTELLIGENCE

Apart from your new sister, the news that has inspired me most in the past month is the launch of Project Arecibo, the first outgoing SETI transmissions in half a century. Two satellites equipped with timeshifting transmitters have started to beam a greeting from humans out toward potentially habitable planets in the nearest fifty star systems. "Nearby," of course, meaning between four and fifty light years away.

The next step in our search for extraterrestrial intelligence has always been to transmit our own messages on a regular basis. But that was put on hold more than fifty years ago, during the War. (Ironically, the original Arecibo telescope that was used for early century SETI collapsed in 2020, an early casualty of extreme weather.)

Young people often question that long-ago decision to avoid outgoing SETI. There were two reasons. First, the priority for science and technology was human survival and the stabilization of our planet's ecosystem. *Terraform Earth!* as the slogan went.

And then there was a second, deeper concern. Suppose our messages *did* reach advanced aliens in some distant star system? And suppose they had the technology to visit us in person?

In the early century, we as a species were in no position to welcome galactic guests. Any advanced extraterrestrial intelligence was certain to see us as immature, destructive primitives who had turned a lovely planet into an orbiting garbage bin.

Those aliens might decide to save us from our unhappy and backward conditions. But human history is not encouraging about the fate of indigenous people when technologically-advanced invaders decide to "save" them. Is that a risk we wanted to volunteer for?

There was another problem with hailing our galactic neighbors in the early century. The vast distances meant that receiving an answer to "Hello" might take, at the very least, years or decades. Not ideal conditions for conducting a getting-to-know-you chat with an alien species.

Now we have quantum timeshifting, a stable planet and, in much of the world, fair and just ways of living. We are a far more united species and better ready to meet what neighbors we might have.

SETI researchers now speculate that timeshifting may be how all mature civilizations communicate in our universe. If so, then all our radio messages sent in the early century must have seemed like the meaningless babble of a one-year-old just learning to speak: not worth serious listening.

With timeshifting, we could theoretically talk with someone in another galaxy, and receive immediate answers.

We could ask some very big questions.

Such as: Has Nous emerged in the evolution of other intelligent lifeforms? Does Nous permeate the universe?

And what do they think happens next?

Maybe we'd even find a solar system with binary suns. Along with a planet where, in my dreams, Marianna and I are still harvesting wild asparagus.

Tuesday, December 18, 2084

Dr. Leah asked for another in-person, and today I made the trek to her Cressville office, almost nine months since the visit that launched this writing project. I asked her in a message whether I should brace myself for bad news.

"Not necessarily. A follow-up is due."

She brought me into her office, rather than one of the sleek examining rooms. I wasn't sure what that meant, except that the chairs are more comfortable.

"So how are you?" she asked as soon as I was seated.

"I'm OK," I said. "Not much change. Except it seems the entire population of New Williamsburg knows I'm thinking about early upholding."

She smiled. "I'm sure that's not true."

"Well," I shrugged. "I don't want to keep secrets from my family. I know they're worried but I'm not going to do anything crazy." I looked at her, perhaps a bit pointedly. "You can tell them I said that."

She ignored the comment. "I haven't seen a lot of change in your monitors. Lately. Although your 7-day moving verbals are consistently lower than they were a year ago."

"I feel something slipping away," I said. "I'm not sure what it is…the sharpness of my thinking? In the document I'm writing, I know I'm rambling. Sometimes, especially later in the day, I can't find the right word."

Dr. Leah nodded. "I've been speaking with Dr. Tenzin and I think we may have an alternative diagnosis for your symptoms. It's somatic symptom disorder, SSD."

This didn't sound good to me. Disease acronyms with consecutive s's are rarely happy news. Too much sibilance.

"It's actually not that common these days. I had to do

some research. In the early century it was seen in perhaps five percent of patients."

"And it is?"

"An old word for it was hypochondria."

I didn't know what to say. "Are you saying I'm making all this up?"

"No, no, not at all. You are really feeling these symptoms. And naturally, they lead you to make conclusions. Even plans." She paused. "Marianna's accident was, what, fifteen years ago?"

"Almost," I said. "I think of her every day."

"Of course you do."

"I didn't start this," I said. "This came from you and my Double, not from me."

"I know. Dr. Tenzin is pretty critical of that. He's not a great fan of algorithmic intuition. In fact, he and I got into a bit of a, ah…discussion…about whether I should have even shared it with you in the first place."

"What is the point of these systems if we don't listen to them?"

She was silent for a moment. "Are you still writing your book?"

"Well," I said, "it's a collection of essays. I'm up to thirty now, so I guess it's long enough to be a book."

"Have you ever written anything this long before?"

"No, never. I like to write freehand but it's always messages to friends or maintenance reports. I kept a journal when I was younger. Now, when I have an idea or something I want to remember, I just tell Domo. But dictating isn't writing."

"You write freehand every day?"

"Of course. I want to get this done while I can, but I'm very slow. So at least seven or eight hours a day. Usually starting in the morning."

"Do you know any other freehand writers who work that much?"

I had to think for a moment. "No, I guess not. When I was studying with Tutor, she arranged for me to practice writing freehand with other students; I would send them little docs and they would write back. But we were only supposed to write two hundred words or so. Tutor had a cute old-fashioned name for the exercise that I can't remember."

Dr. Leah smiled slightly. "Was it 'pen pal'?"

"That's it."

She looked down at her pad. "And you never use autoparser? As I recall, you hate autoparser."

"Not hate—it helps a lot of people. But I don't want to use it."

"Okay," she said finally. "I think what you're feeling, and what the monitors are picking up, is natural mental exhaustion. Writing freehand for extended periods is very tiring. It's unnatural, especially for those who learned later in life."

"You're kidding me."

"I'm not. Think about it. If you wanted to cross a big lake, you could take a power boat. Or you could row. If you rowed yourself that far, no matter how well you trained, your arms and shoulder muscles would be exhausted when you got to the other side. If we ran you through a two-minute upper-body coordination scan right after you finished rowing, your numbers would not be good."

"So I'm doing this to myself?"

"We still don't know exactly what triggered the initial alert from your Double. Dr. Tenzin calls it an algorithmic fart, which is not a technical term. But the alert has been maintained by these extended bouts of freehand writing. Your Double must only have a very small sample of patients who do this sort of sustained activity."

"So maybe I should take a break from the writing?"

"Consider it a sabbatical."

Wednesday December 19

I left, not quite relieved. Is Dr. Leah trying to distract me with this alternative explanation, some behavioral therapy to sooth my thoughts and deter me from any rash behavior?

It has now been nine months since the first alert from my Double. Following Dr. Leah's advice, I've taken a week off from my writing. Although it may be coincidence, my seven-day average verbals went up. Perhaps this is significant, or maybe just some form of remission.

It seems as if the last months have passed so quickly, since we stood together on the riverbank on 350 Day and tossed your wishes. Tomorrow we'll all be together again, for Winter Solstice; there will be the customary public celebration in town center. There's also a Chardinist service in late afternoon, and then I'll go to your house for dinner and gifts.

You've been excited about Solstice Day for weeks; someday you'll be surprised to learn it's only been around for the last 50 years or so. It started as a somewhat fringy combination of planetary respect and anti-consumerism, first among Pagans and then more broadly. Now I think Solstice overshadows Christmas (except among Christians, of course), especially for children. After all, what kid wouldn't want to get their December gift a few days early?

I am looking forward to it all. It seems as if the year has passed very quickly. In the days since my appointment with Dr. Leah I've had some good conversations with your parents, and Mena.

I've also reread these pages with a fresh mind. I'm not sure I have a great deal more to say—in fact, I have already gone on far too long, although I know you would be patient.

Somehow I managed to veer off the path of essay. I did not intend this to be an autobiography, or to reminisce about, say, the Dr. Denton intimates kit we bought for your father when he was 15. You certainly don't need to hear the details of my relationship with Mena, wherever that may be headed. At times, I've found myself having a very adult conversation with a five-year-old. That has to be a symptom of something.

This text needs a good trimming. And then I will print these words on natural paper. Expensive, but in the end there's still nothing like the feel of a natural sheet, compared to even the best active. I think your fingertips can sense a continuum stretching back to green swaths of papyrus growing in the shallows of the Nile.

Or maybe not. There was an early century saying you'll never understand: "That's not worth the paper it's printed on." The phrase was meant to deride the words themselves, implying that they had even less value than the paper, which was then so cheap as to seem almost worthless.

Natural paper was a great display device back then: cheap, no batteries, highly portable, recyclable. But it was terrible for transport or storage. In the early century much of the world was drowning in vast quantities of disorganized paper. Even health records were on paper!

Natural paper, however, is still a connection to the past. When you read these words, you will know I touched these pages as well.

I'll have the pages bound into an actual book—we have a talented second-generation bookbinder in New Williamsburg. She travels every year to Monterey, in California, to choose the best sides of kelp leather; her bindings are beautiful.

At the very least, these pages should be a memorable object.

You're too young, of course, to receive this now; perhaps for your 18th birthday? Or sooner, if it becomes necessary. But whatever my Double saw looming in the future may be more distant than I initially feared. Maybe I will be able to tell you about this century in person, rather than through these pages.

And of course I look forward to seeing your little sister. Dylan and Sofia have already told me her name: Marianna.

I will do one thing with this text right now. It will be the payload in my timeshifting experiments. I've finished the email spoofing software, and I need to return the timeshifting chip to AgBot next week. (The chips are very expensive and regulated under the Temporal Research laws.) I've mulled using these words as a test vehicle since the day I started to work with the chip.

I don't quite know why I want to do this. When I told Mena about it the other night, she said maybe it's because with the proper education in the early century, I might have become a writer. Now, perhaps, I can feel like I was.

But who knows? This experiment is like tossing a message in a bottle into an extremely large ocean, without knowing exactly where the ocean is. No one may ever read this. If it does wash up on some shore, who knows what tattered condition these words may be in?

Mena, ever practical, asked me: if someone in the past actually does read this, am I worried about violating the timeshifting regulations?

Not really.

The law reads that we "may not interfere with historical

processes." No chance of that. No one in the early century will believe a word of this. They'll consider it a fantasy, altogether impossible. Believe me on that; I was there.

So I will send this email artifact out later today, with no qualms. Even if no one in the early century ever sees it, I will feel as if I've left this little book on some timeless shelf.

Before I do that, I'm going to write out a few thoughts for my toast at Solstice Day dinner, when I will join you and your parents tomorrow.

Mena is coming with me tomorrow. This year we will toast you, Luca, and your sister-to-be.

And also the future.

Posted November 4, 2020

Update: Email from the Future?

Aldus found me. Or rather, his parents did. This morning, to be precise. After two weeks, someone forwarded my posting of the "TXT" document to them.

I heard from his parents right away; they are extremely angry. The personal details in the document, it turns out, are all correct: They are educators, their child is ten years old, they live in Park Slope, and so on.

They initially assumed that I was the author of the piece, but, once everyone calmed down a bit, I think I convinced them otherwise.

His parents have no idea who might have gone to the trouble of writing so lengthy a document. Not all of the personal details could have been culled from their Facebook pages, although they nonetheless deactivated their accounts.

The parents won't take legal action as long as I stop sharing the document. So I'll be removing the link shortly. I see that about twenty sites currently link to the page; rather than leaving a broken link, I'll replace it with a brief message explaining that the document has been removed for copyright reasons.

And, dear readers, if you downloaded a copy, please delete it as well.

There's no reason for young Aldus ever to be bothered with any of this.

ACKNOWLEDGMENTS

My thanks to April Smith, Jann Wenner, Vernon Church, Sarah Lazin, Catharine Strong, Roger Fidler and MJ Buchanan for their patient reading—and rereading—and all the good counsel that resulted.

And to Donna Rini, uncompromising in her art, who always reminds me to stay true.

* * *

Michael Rogers
New York City
January 2022

ABOUT THE AUTHOR

MICHAEL ROGERS is an author, technology pioneer and futurist, who most recently served as futurist-in-residence for The New York Times. He has worked with companies ranging from FedEx, Boeing and NBC Universal to Microsoft, Pfizer and Siemens, focusing on how companies can think about the future in useful ways. He speaks to audiences worldwide and is a regular guest on radio and television.

Rogers began his career as a writer for Rolling Stone magazine. He co-founded Outside magazine and then launched Newsweek's technology column, winning numerous journalism awards. For ten years he was vice president of The Washington Post Company's new media division, leading both the newspaper and Newsweek into the new century and earning patents for multimedia technology.

He is also a best-selling novelist whose books have been published worldwide, chosen for Book-of-the-Month club, and optioned for film.

Rogers studied physics and creative writing at Stanford University, with additional studies in finance and management at the Stanford Business School Executive Program. He divides his time between New York City and Sicily.

For more information or to inquire about speaking:
www.michaelrogers.com

Photo: © Donna Rini

Made in the USA
Columbia, SC
11 July 2023

20275231R00152